LOU GRIMES

Chicago 45

LARRY & SHIRLEY CRANDELL

Authors of:

Tony Simons Series

Lou Grimes Series

Available on Amazon

Larry & Shirley Crandell

Copyright © 2020 by Larry and Shirley Crandell. All Rights Reserved. No reproductions in whole or in part without permission.

This is a work of fiction. All incidents and dialogue and all characters, with the exception of some well-known historical figures, are products of the author's imagination and are not to be construed as real. Where real-life historical figures appear, the situations, incidents and dialogues concerning those persons are entirely fictional and are not intended to depict actual events or to change the entirely fictional nature of the work. In all other respects, any resemblance to actual persons, living or dead, businesses, companies, events or locales is entirely coincidental and are either the product of the author's imagination or are used fictitiously.

Publishers Larry & Shirley Crandell 2020

ISBN 978-1-7771693-0-5

Edited by: Kathryn Crandell and Garry & Brenda Boese

Cover Image by: Stokkete/Shutterstock.com

Acknowledgement

To my loving wife Shirley who has been my rock and strongest supporter over the years in my struggle to make sense of all the strange ramblings running around in my head and put them to paper.

She has been the one who constantly puts my wheels back on track and is my calming influence when I stray into the weird and unknown territory that is my imagination.

She makes it all flow in a straight line and in the end even I believe the stories.

I could never do this without her nor would I want to.

Your loving husband and biggest fan, thank you!

PART I

Lou Grimes

Chapter 1

Chicago 45

The city whose name is taken from the American Indian word for "Smelly Onion or Swamp Grass" finally started trying to clean up its image but it had taken 30 years to get this far and many lives had been destroyed. World War II was just coming to an end and men were looking for work and a release from the hell they had endured. It was a dark memory that never seemed to want to let go but Lou Grimes, ex-Chicago Police Detective, was trying very hard to put it in the past.

Lou's life started with the promise of a bright future for the 19 year old innocent in the Chicago Police Department in 1915. He was the happiest young man in Chicago that bright sunny Monday morning when he pinned on his badge, #452.

It was so long ago now, 30 years today. A life time of hard work and trying to make a difference brought him to where he was now. He was tall, about six feet, with tired droopy red eyes and big jowls, his ears were oversized and he had a bit of a paunch. His hair was dark, but it was starting to gray at the temple and he needed it cut. He wore the same old brown hat and gray open trench coat he had worn for years, along with baggy pants and worn out shoes because that's all he had.

Disillusioned with his life, he sat on his bar stool at Eddie's on 8th, his local hangout. He was quietly humming "Happy Birthday" to himself, all the while looking down into his beer, remembering his past.

Today really was Lou Grime's birthday and he wondered to himself if he had just pissed his life away or had it all been worth it? He could still remember his first day in uniform. It had been raining for three days, like it does in Chicago sometimes and even though it had been more than 60 years since that famous fire tried to burn the city down, it could remind you when you least expected it to. If you were outside on a damp morning, in the right place at the right time back then, and the wind was blowing just so, you could catch a faint smell of burning creosote oil in the air.

Construction was still going on even today and the scarred remains of some of the old buildings were still standing as a testament of harder times.

Lou sat alone on his favorite barstool and reached back into his memory thirty years before. He could still taste it. He could still hear his training Sergeant, Terry O'Dell, telling him of the two dark days the devil himself visited Chicago.

It was October 1871 when dry weather and an abundance of wooden buildings along the streets and sidewalks made Chicago vulnerable to fires. Legend holds that the blaze started when a family cow knocked over a lighted lantern however, Catherine O'Leary denied the charge and the true cause of the fire had never been determined. The fire killed 300 people, destroyed roughly 3.3 square miles and left 100,000 people homeless. "Those were dark, dark, days," he'd say.

Lou loved walking the streets of Chicago back then. He was proud of what he was doing and in his mind, making a difference. He knew the streets like the back of his hand. He grew up in these neighborhoods and people knew him and his parents, liked them and respected what he had become. His parents had come here earlier in the century following a dream.

Chicago had always been the Mecca of the Midwest. Farm boys, even though warned, left the fields for the wickedness of the city where heavy industry churned out steel and other raw materials that fueled America's growing prosperity.

Young women from small towns outside Chicago came to the city looking for sales jobs in the big grand department stores, Marshal Fields and Carson Scott which were still standing. This was their dream.

It was happier times for Grimes back then, before the shit hit the fan and reality showed him what life was really about, as a flat foot in Chicago.

Lou came back to reality for a minute and ordered another beer and rubbed his three day old beard.

"What are you humming Lou?" Eddie the bartender asked as he came closer.

Eddie Flannigan was second generation Irish-American but still had ties to the old country and had a bit of the Irish brogue when he was provoked. He wasn't a tall man, but what he lacked in height he made up in ferocity. His limp came from street fighting in his younger day. He inherited his curly red hair from his old man. He had taken over the bar when his father passed away, almost a decade ago.

Lou thought for a second and answered his friend and favorite tap puller in a voice low enough so no one else could hear "it's my god damned birthday today Eddie," he said spitting out a piece of cigar. I'm forty goddamn nine."

"No shit!" Eddie replied in a booming voice and a big grin. "Happy birthday you old bastard, this one's on the house," as he planted a cold draft next to Lou and took his empty glass. Eddie moved away and looked back over his shoulder and asked "did you eat today birthday boy?"

"Had a hot dog at Saul's," he growled.

Saul Gronski was one of Chicago's icons. He had once been a big time banker on Wall Street back in the day but when people began to jump off buildings because they had lost everything in the market crash, Saul changed professions. Now he sold the best hot dogs in Chicago, just outside Palisades Park Race Track and was a wealth of information for Lou when it came to who was doing what in town and to whom.

Lou ate there almost every day and Saul would ramble on like an old woman as he stood with hot coffee in one hand and the best hot dog he ever ate in the other.

"Keep them coming until I fall off this seat, Eddie or can't remember what I'm humming."

It all began to show itself for Constable Grimes four years into what he thought was a great career with a promising future. He was doing his job and loving it, keeping the peace, having run-ins with local drunks and doing raids on whore houses along with the odd robbery. It was all good stuff, but nothing had prepared Grimes for what was showing itself on the horizon.

Chicago was the scene of a vicious race riot in 1919, between African Americans who lived on the south side and European immigrants on the north side.

Lou remembered it being called "the great migration." Hundreds of thousands of African Americans left the Deep South in search of opportunity in the northern city of Chicago. Factory jobs were plentiful at first for the waves of immigrants who had made it there, but harmony changed to hate and hate to violence among the various groups of ethnic and cultural diversities.

Seventy-seven different neighborhoods were competing for the same jobs and the same housing. It came to be known as "Red Summer," meaning "bloody summer." It was a dark stain on the history of the city that had been the envy of the east coast.

It started innocently enough, that warm, sunny Saturday afternoon, July 27, 1919. It was like the entire population of Chicago had converged on the beach to escape the waves of heat that were choking the city.

A young African boy was leisurely swimming just off shore in Lake Michigan in his "designated swimming area," when he accidently drifted into an area reserved for "whites only."

He was noticed right away, stoned and eventually drowned. When the police refused to arrest the white man that started the incident, crowds began to gather on the beach and the disturbance began.

Lou and twenty other policemen were sent to the beach to calm things down, but it was useless. Rumors swept the city as fighting broke out between gangs and mobs of both races. It kept getting worse and for thirteen days and nights, Chicago was a war zone and Grimes was right in the middle of it. He stood shoulder to shoulder with the Illinois National Guard, squaring off with angry groups of people that only the day before they had called friends. Now they were angry mobs and animals that wanted blood and could not be controlled.

Grimes had been seen by them to be the "white enemy" in uniform. It was the scariest moment in his short career. By the end of the riots, fighting and burning, Lou was told that 38 people had died; 23 blacks and 15 whites. There were also 537 injured and a thousand black families were left homeless.

At 23 years old, Constable Grimes had become a seasoned Chicago Policeman and had seen the black in men's souls when they were backed up against the wall. It had hardened Lou to this very day.

Lou recalled, at the start of 1920 the government banned the making, sale and consumption of alcohol. Chicago said no. Alcohol manufacturers moved underground to warehouses and homes giving rise to "bathtub gin and bootleggers." Alcohol sales continued in illegal taverns called "speakeasies," and Lou was involved in the destruction of hundreds of these houses that had proliferated in the city.

He had been briefed that Al Capone had control of 10,000 Speakeasies in Chicago and raked in some $70,000,000 a year. You could always get a drink in Chicago, no matter how hard the police tried to stop it.

Lou remembered those lawless days clearly but he had to smile a bit. The speakeasies, burlesque shows and jazz clubs were warm memories for Lou, but the rivalry between the Capone gang on the south side and George "Bugsy" Moran's gang on the north side never slowed down.

Back then, the twenty's were the golden age of Chicago. Grimes remembered listening to Bill McFarlane and the Chicago Horns play at the "Green Mill," a jazz club where

Al Capone used to hang out, but Lou had not met him at that time. For white Americans, it meant going to cabarets to hear African American musicians play a new kind of music called jazz. Chicago would become a fertile ground for jazz greats such as Duke Ellington, Louie Armstrong and Bessie Smith. Lou listened to them all.

Chicago thrived and survived the twenties no matter what. Grimes couldn't remember not being so busy. There was always something going on.

In 1929, when he thought gang wars were bad and things couldn't get any worse, they did. The stock market crashed, sending thousands to their deaths and crime soared. Prohibition supporters and the leading voice in the anti-alcohol movement, the "Women's Christian Temperance Movement," was based just outside of Chicago and they marched on city hall and the mayor's office en masse constantly.

Lou found himself on the line facing these angry ladies often and wasn't sure how to handle them, they were tough. The ladies found they were alone in this quest but marched thousands at a time until they were finally heard.

One of the worst days Lou ever had was when he had to arrest a fellow policeman that he knew well, for bribery. The man called himself a "Social Associate," whatever that meant Lou thought. He was very closely associated with the mob, he admitted and liked it. Lou found out that he was so close that Al Capone had given his friend a case of expensive champagne one Christmas and racing tips at the track with twenty to one odds, guaranteed to win.

Lou had met Capone once. They had raided a speakeasy on the south side and Capone was there partying. Neither of the men spoke to each other. Lou just watched Capone being lead away, laughing and telling people that he'd be back in an hour and the champagne should be kept cold.

On Thursday, February 14, the next morning, Lou and a dozen police officers raced to 2122 North Clark Street to a warehouse garage at Dickinson and Clark in the area of Lincoln Park. It was Valentine's Day 1929. Seven members and associates of Chicago's north side gang were murdered. The men were gathered at the garage on that fateful morning, lined up against the wall and shot by four unknown assailants that were dressed like policemen.

The police denied being involved and later found that members of Egan Rats Gang were working for Capone and were guilty of the horror that Lou would never forget.

He remembered back when the city permitted vice and corruption. It lived and thrived on it, even the police were taking their cut by looking away. Grimes hated this practice.

The police force was what he cared about and arresting these gangsters is what he lived for.

He didn't drink or gamble back then, but he did like to dance. They had Taxi Dance Halls, Grimes remembered them fondly. For a Dime a dance a patron could dance up close with a scantily clad woman. They played one chorus of music and you paid a dime, so you had to buy a whole roll of tickets to keep her in your arms.

Grimes smiled as he slipped into a popular song of the day under his breath. "Ten cents a dance, baby; ten cents a dance, mmmmm mmmmmmm mmmm."

He should have known better but that's where he met and married Trixie. She was everything a man could want and at the time, Lou Grimes wanted her, bad. As he thought back on it, it was probably a mistake. Things have a way of working themselves out. He smiled to himself, "after twelve years, she was Ralph's problem now."

He remembered catching them in bed together and how she screamed at him to get out and that Ralph was a better man than he would ever be.

He remembered walking out of the flat and never looking back.

He saw his supervisor Ralph Potter, at work the next day and landed a six-week suspension for walking up to the asshole and punching him in the mouth sending him over his desk where he laid unconscious on the floor. This action eventually led to Lou's resignation and retirement. That had only been two months ago.

He grasped another ribbon in his memory and remembered the start of World War II and how desperately he wanted to enlist and do his part. He was a seasoned veteran in the Chicago Police Department of some twenty five years but he practically ran down to the recruiting office and stood in line for hours with hundreds of men looking to enlist.

He passed all the initial requirements but when it came to the physical he was listed "4F" because he had flat feet. It was a crushing blow.

Lou snapped back into reality and remembered where he was. He got a warm feeling inside and calm came over him. He was in Eddie's. He got up from his stool and weaved his way through the crowd. "Where in the world had they come from?" he thought. "To hell with them he grumbled, he didn't need people, he needed to piss."

The men's room was full. "What the hell," he thought. "Are we having a meeting in here or something?" He looked at the men lined up at the urinals. "Stop playing with yourselves," he said "and let a man take a leak."

His bladder was screaming at him when he finally made it to a stall. When he looked down to finish, he noticed his hand was all scratched and bruised. "What the hell," he said again to himself.

He again weaved through the people in the bar that had not been there before. "Where the hell did they all come from?" he thought. "What time is it anyway?" He made it back safely to his stool and looked down at his hand once more. "How the hell did that happen?" He didn't remember falling or anything. Lou finally shrugged it off and got comfortable on his favorite stool. "Happy birthday to me!" he mumbled.

It was not much later in the evening and for some reason or other, Eddie's was filling up with customers, loud customers; drinking, laughing, noisy customers.

Lou was quietly minding his own business, sipping his beer when he became aware of the seat next to him being occupied. He didn't want any company, but what could he do?

He glanced over to his left to see a middle-aged woman had sat down next to him and lit a cigarette. Lou noticed right away that the dame was trying to look younger than she was, much younger and had done a bad job of it. Her dress was too tight and too short and fit her badly, rolling out in all the wrong places. She had too much makeup on and wore dark red lipstick and fingernails along with some kind of hat.

Lou could see right away that she was drunk and he was about to be hit on, which he didn't need. She was smoking this long narrow cigarette and Lou knew she thought this was attractive until the long ash fell off and dropped on the bar in front of him.

"How about you buy a lady a drink, handsome?"

Lou slowly glanced over at her, looked at the ashes on the bar and then back to his unwelcome visitor. "Listen to me you old broad," he said in a low voice. "I'm not looking for company and I'm sure as hell not buying you a drink."

The painted-on smile drained from her face as she rose from the stool, smashed the cigarette out in the ashtray and looked right at Lou. "I can see why you're sitting here alone, slick. You've got a nasty disposition and a face that looks like a moose." With that she was gone and immediately hitting on another unsuspecting patron.

"Do you want another beer, birthday boy?" Eddie yelled over.

Lou waved him in and as Eddie sat the beer down, Lou looked up at him and asked "Eddie, do I have a face that looks like a moose?"

"Oh hell Lou," Eddie replied. "What do I know? I just sling beer."

It was two in the morning and the place was finally quiet again. Eddie was going about his business of closing up the bar by emptying ashtrays and putting the chairs up on the tables. Once this was done he wandered over to his friend and put his hand on Lou's shoulder. "Time to go home, birthday boy; I'm closing up."

Lou wasn't sure he could move, let alone get up and walk across the street, but he managed to do both. In true Chicago form, it was raining again and he was soaked by the time he reached his home, the Biltmore Boarding House.

It was an old brick brownstone, two-story building, built in the late 1800's and it was run by an old Polish woman named Ruth.

Ruth had had a rough life in Poland. She had married young to an older man, a farmer, had four children and immigrated to the USA, eventually arriving in Chicago at the turn of the century. They scraped money together from their farm and bought the Biltmore because it was dirt cheap, falling down and was about to be torn down.

Hard work by the family restored the building to a point so that people could live there and things were beginning to look up until tragedy struck and Ruth's husband was an accident victim of a drive by shooting the year before. It was hard for Ruth after that. The building was always in need of repair and money was tight. The children were now grown and gone and Ruth was feeling her age. Only time would tell if she would be able to continue.

The Brownstone was located right across the street from Eddie's and Lou liked it that way, especially on nights like this. For $5 a week Lou was renting a 10 x 12 room with creaky wooden floors. It was furnished, if you could call it that. There was an old double bed that sagged deep in the middle where over the years the springs had seen too much action.

The room also had a small table and chair pushed up next to the window, a well aged, over-stuffed chair and a pole lamp that didn't work. He had complained repeatedly to Ruth about it, but it was still not working.

The light from the window was all he had and in the daytime it was fine but at night the flashing lights from the street could not be controlled because the blind wasn't working either. The most valuable thing in his room was his two burner hotplate that Eddie had given to him when he moved in because he knew Lou's situation. He could boil coffee or burn toast whenever he wanted.

He barely made it upstairs to the second floor and fought with the lock on his door for five minutes before he could enter his room, take off his hat and shoes and flop onto his mattress face down, singing one more time "Happy birthday to me."

Chapter 2

Lou realized quickly that keeping things simple was much better than complicating his day with unnecessary bullshit. Simple routine was his way of life now.

He came alive about 10 AM to the sounds of the world outside his window and the streets below. Cars were driving by at breakneck speeds of 20 mph. Streetcars were ringing their bells, people were moving garbage cans and yelling from open windows to people down below about absolutely nothing at all that Lou wanted to hear.

The rain had stopped some time during the night and life on 8th Street, July 7, 1945 in Chicago, USA was about to begin for him.

A fresh breeze blew into Lou's room from the outside. The air was cleaner in the morning after a rain, but would soon turn heavy with humidity as the heat of the day started to bounce off the buildings and the dust from the streets rose up to choke your lungs and make your eyes water.

Right now, he just welcomed the breeze. The sounds outside his window were amplified ten-fold by the pounding in his head and that unknown nasty taste in his mouth. He rubbed his eyes, trying to clear the crap that had gathered there and noted that his three day old beard would last another day.

He needed coffee badly, but right now that would have to wait, he needed to piss now!

He did not have the luxury of a bathroom in his 10 x 12 palace. That beauty was down the hall about twenty feet and was used commonly between eight other people on the floor. Lou never knew what to expect each time he opened the bathroom door.

The occupants on his floor were less than house broken and Lou was sure they had never learned how to use a toilet, let alone flush it. The odd time he found the room empty he had to clean everything thoroughly before attempting anything. Then there was that fun little thing he had to do to flush the toilet. He had to take the lid off the back and fish the chain out of the water, if there was a chain there at all. "Life in the Biltmore," he thought "nothing like it."

He put his shoes back on and walked down the hall. The floor was damp and sticky. "You just don't know," he thought. Down the hall he shuffled in all his finery from the night before. He grabbed the door knob and rattled it and found it locked.

"Occupied!" someone growled from behind the door.

Lou called out loud, so the occupant could hear him "don't forget to flush, asshole!"

He could only guess what was happening in there and didn't want any part of it. He turned around, shuffled back down the hall to his room to use his emergency whisky bottle. Lou had played this game before.

It was already a quarter past ten before he stepped out of his room, turned and tried to lock his door. In doing so he glanced down "what the hell was wrong with his hand?" It was bruised and scratched up and swollen. Did he punch a wall the previous night during his birthday celebration? It was all an aching haze that could only be cured by black coffee and a handful of aspirin.

He was having trouble with his lock again, it barely worked at all. It needed to be replaced and Ruth was going to hear about it.

Lou headed down the stairs and was making for the front door to begin a routine that he had made for himself over the last couple of months since he left the police force.

Phase one of his routine was to walk down the block to the corner of 8th and Wells and pick up his morning newspaper and today's racing form. Before grabbing the doorknob and opening the outside door he looked back and saw Ruth sweeping the hallway. "When are you going to get the lamp in my room fixed?" he piped up, "and the damn door lock is sticking again. How many times do I have to ask? I'm a paying customer here, Ruthie. Get the lead out!"

Ruth looked up from her task and answered blandly, "I heard you before, and I'll get to it. Keep your shirt on!"

Lou was coming to the realization that he liked bugging his landlady. It was another thing that got his day started on the right foot. He enjoyed starting his day this way.

The newsstand was operated by Benny, a World War II Veteran that had seen too much action and had been injured when they stormed the beach at Juno. Word was that a shell had exploded near his foxhole on the beach and the concussion rattled something loose in his head. Now, it was a challenge for him to speak and not twitch. His twitching became more exaggerated when he got excited and so did his stutter.

Lou liked visiting Benny every day. He knew he appreciated the company and also knew that Benny watched what was going on in the neighborhood and had a keen ear for listening to people talk. Everyone likes to talk around a newsstand. Benny was a wealth of information and also gave Lou a few tips on the horses he had heard.

"L-L-L Lou," Benny stammered and smiled as he rose from his little chair off to the side.

"Morning Benny," Lou replied. "Paper and a track form please."

Benny was middle-aged and slightly built. He walked with a distinct limp. His hair was salt and pepper and his eyes were green when you could see them because he never focused on anything.

Lou had been coming to Benny for the last couple of months and knew he had what he wanted. Besides, he thought, it was a good way to get Benny talking.

Benny handed over the papers, collected his nickel and struck up a conversation. "Hey L-Lou," he stuttered, "have you n-n noticed a lot of guys seemed to be h-hanging out d down Walker's Street near the old fabric warehouse? There's a lot of activity there, for a p-p-place that's supposed to b-b-be empty. Cars always speed b-by me early in the m morning and in the evening, heading to and f-from that location."

Lou said that he hadn't noticed but when he had the time, he'd have a look. He thanked Benny for the papers and the news and was just walking away when Benny looked out his stand and yelled "H-h-h happy b-b birthday, Lou. Oh, b-b-by the way, L-Lou," Benny continued, "for what it's w-worth b-b-buddy, I don't think you look like a m-m-moose either!"

"Jesus Christ," Lou muttered to himself, "is nothing sacred around here?"

Before returning to his room, he stopped at Lenny's smoke shop. The conversation there was always interesting and he would buy another one of his favorites, a five cent Cuban cigar that he'd smoke all day.

Lenny was an immigrant from Cuba. He was a short, mature gentleman. He sported a paunch that he said was due to his wife's cooking. He always came over to his customers and shook their hands when they arrived. He was always more than happy to divulge the secrets involved in making a good cigar.

After his visit with Lenny, Lou returned to his room for the second phase of his familiar routine. He made a pot of strong black coffee and sat at his table catching the breeze, looking out his window from time to time to see what was going on, while reading his paper and studying the race form.

He was starting to think about what he could do to bring in a little more dough, which is why he had the paper. That was for later. Today was the day his horse was going to win. All he had to do was pick it!

At a quarter past noon Lou headed for the third phase of his routine, the track. This was where he would buy the best hotdog in the world, at his favorite stand and talk to his favorite vendor, Saul. He could smell the roasting hotdogs at least a half block before he got there. His mouth watered and he could almost taste the six inches of freshly ground heaven, rolled up in a home-made bun that Saul's wife had baked that morning. He could imagine squirting the yellow gold over the hot round steak and topping it off with onions and peppers, then his first bite.

Saul was a slender Jewish man and although he was no longer a banker, he still dressed in a dark suit and tie that had seen better days. He was a proud man and Lou could tell that he was just as proud in his new profession cooking hot dogs as he had been as a banker. He wore round, wire-framed glasses propped on his nose and had a pocket watch with a chain.

Saul would catch him up on what was going on in Chicago that morning and then he would head through the turnstiles into the massive building and up to the betting windows with a bag of fresh roasted peanuts and five dollars to make his fortune. Today was the day, he just knew it.

Lou could probably have walked into this place blindfolded and still know where he was and where to place a bet. He knew the people there, what they were doing and what they were hoping to do.

Everyone had a system or a lucky rabbit's foot or a hot tip that a friend had given them and Lou was no different. He always bet the long-shots. In his mind, the law of averages was on his side. The nag he bet on had to eventually win.

He liked coming to the track, to him it was his second home. He liked the people there, the smell of a thousand different cigars and most of all, the horses. He also knew what was about to happen and smiled to himself.

Stella was about to give him hell. He walked up to his lucky betting window, number 9 and was confronted by his conscience, Stella. She was in her mid-forties, with blond, medium length curly hair, dark red lips and nail polish to match. Today she was wearing a white, long sleeved cotton shirt with large cuffs and the shirt was buttoned all the way to her neck.

She reminded Lou of a movie actress he saw at the pictures some time back, Jean Harlow. He had a "thing" for Jean Harlow and a warm spot inside of him for Stella.

He blinked back to reality and found himself standing in front of her with nothing to say. With pursed lips she leaned forward as he got to the wicket. "With all the money you lose at this track, Lou, you could probably get yourself a new coat."

"What fun would that be darlin," he teased. "I'd miss coming here to see your smiling face and giving you my hard-earned cash every day."

Stella had to admit to herself secretly that she'd miss his mug if he stopped showing up. "What are we playing today, slick?" she teased.

"Lady B in the sixth," Lou said and handed her the five dollar bill.

Stella took a deep breath and let it out slowly, "at least give yourself a fighting chance Lou," she sighed, "Lady B? Really? That nag is twenty to one and hasn't seen the finish line first since Taft was President."

"I know," Lou said excitedly, "today is her day I've just got a feeling. Really Stella, when this horse wins, I'm going to take you to dinner at the fanciest club in town."

She had seen that look in his eyes before, so there was no trying to change his mind. She took the five, gave him his stub and wished him well.

He gave her a wink as he walked away and she thought for a second "maybe today is the day, maybe."

The sixth race was still a half hour away, but Lou liked to come early. It gave him a chance to relax a little, eat his peanuts and look around to see who was there and what was happening.

The usual people were there along with a couple of bookies that were watching to see if their suckers would win so they could get paid and a couple of knee breakers making sure debts were collected. It was just another day at the track.

Lou recognized Geno, the baker with his wife and tipped his hat. A couple of guys he played cards with were there and Whitie Simms was sitting a couple of seats in front of them. Whitie was short, thin and bony, his hair was white, hence the nickname "Whitie." He tended to whine a lot. Whitie was a low-level thief that lived with his mother over on 4th Street. When Lou was still in the police force, he busted Whitie a couple of times for possession of stolen property, but nothing really serious. One thing was for sure with Whitie, he couldn't pick a winning horse to save his soul, so Lou was in good company.

The fifth race went off without a hitch and Lou saw Whitie throw his losing tickets into the air and walk away. Geno's wife must have won because she was jumping in the air so hard, her hat was falling off.

The sixth race was getting ready to go and like usual, Lou was getting this sick feeling in the pit of his stomach. Nerves and anticipation were taking over. He was already seeing his life change before his eyes as Lady B came across the finish line first.

The starting gate crashed open and the horses exploded from their stalls, clawing at the ground and the air, trying to run away from the pack. The sound of their hooves hitting the dirt was deafening. They moved around the track faster and faster as the colorful little jockeys on their backs held on for dear life and hit the horses with their crops. A whirlwind of mud in the air, colored sashes and animals came to the wire all at once to produce a photo finish.

Lou didn't have to worry about photographs because Lady B came in dead last, some twenty lengths behind the second last horse. His momentary excitement changed to that numb feeling you get when you're going home empty handed and no one gives a damn.

He went by Stella's wicket and smiled a sad smile, winked at her and put his head down. "Maybe tomorrow will be better," he told himself. As he passed her, she wanted to reach out and give him a hug, but that wasn't going to happen, not today anyway.

The afternoon had gone by quickly and Lou's stomach was starting to act up because Saul's hotdog was long gone and he still had four more blocks to walk before he got back to his neighborhood.

The smell of dinners cooking was coming from open kitchen windows and it filled the air. The kids playing outside near their homes would soon be called in and men would be getting home from work.

Lou was familiar with this route; he used it many times in the last couple of months and knew he still had the better part of a mile to go before he reached his street.

This was the time of day that Lou liked to be with his thoughts, particularly what had happened over the last year. He was happier now, he knew that. He liked his new group of friends and his routine, but he knew that he would have to scare up a few more bucks in order to keep the wolf from his door. That was something to think about tomorrow, right now, Maude's Diner was calling.

He couldn't think of anything that he wanted to change with the routine he had set for himself; no questions, no surprises, just the next thing and the next thing right now was dinner.

A block over from Eddie's, Maude's Diner was an old railway car that had been converted into a diner at the turn of the century and was owned by Bass and Maude Stockman.

Bass's father had worked for the railway and when he retired he purchased the old dining car that was scheduled to be scrapped and he turned it into a place to eat.

Bass worked in the Diner with his father until he took it over by himself twenty years before. It was just a place to eat back then but it took on a reputation of its own when Bass married Maude and things really took off. She could cook like an angel and filled the Diner and the immediate area around it with the wonderful smells of home cooking and the best baking you could find anywhere.

Walking into Maude's in the early morning you would be greeted by fresh brewed coffee and the sizzling smell of bacon and eggs was heaven. You never wanted to leave.

The Diner was famous in the neighborhood. Lou was aware of this and more and tonight he was going to treat himself to the house special, liver and onions, mashed potatoes, peas, coffee and a big piece of Maude's famous Pecan pie! It was the best $1.05 you could ever spend.

He came through the door of the Diner and was immediately engulfed by the smells of her wonderful cooking. He rarely took his Fedora off anywhere, but this place deserved respect.

Maude saw him coming in and waved him over to his favorite booth. She reminded Lou of a favorite old aunt, always fussing around. She was about Lou's age, but shorter and a little heavier and wore glasses. She was always in an apron with her hair tied back and covered with a net. Bass called her "his diamond in the rough and when God made Maude, he threw away the mold."

She came up to Lou's table and gave him a hug before he sat down. "What's all this about Maude?" he asked

"Happy Birthday you old goat!" she said. "Where were you yesterday? I baked you a small cake with a candle," she smiled. "Truth be told, it was more like a muffin."

Lou said "I'm sorry Maude but I got held up at Eddie's and things happen and how did you know it was my birthday?"

"Word gets around Lou," she said.

He sat down and shook his head in disbelief, but also smiled a bit too. "Give me the special Maude," he piped up, "I'm starving." Lou loved Maude's liver and onions.

She brought him over the evening paper and a hot cup of coffee before she hurried off to make his meal and he settled in happily waiting for what he knew would be a feast. Maude did not disappoint, every bite was better than the last and before he knew it he was wiping the plate clean with a piece of home-made bread.

Maude came back with more coffee and a massive piece of Pecan pie and as she put the pie down in front of him she said "the meal is paid for Lou, no charge."

Lou was taken aback for a moment and looked at Maude with questioning eyes. Maude just smiled, "old Mrs. Gardiner was in here yesterday for tea, as she does, and mentioned that you had taken care of an asshole cabbie that was working the area and was speeding up his meter on the old people because they didn't know better. She said she told you what was happening and you told her not to worry, that you would take care of it. She told me your next meal was on her and thanks."

The lights came on in Lou's memory and he now knew how he hurt his hand. It came from slamming it into the cabbie's face and ramming the guys head into the steering wheel. He thanked Maude for the great meal and tried to pay anyway but she put his hat on his head and pushed him out the door.

"Don't be a stranger Lou Grimes," she said as he moved down the street to begin the final phase of his schedule, Eddie's. His stool was calling him and a few cold beers would round out his day and put an end to the mystery of his injured hand.

Eddie's was Lou Grime's safe space. Everybody needs a place to go where you can just hang out and play some pool, darts or a card game. For Lou, this was Eddie's on 8th. It was another old Brownstone two-story building that was in Chicago's earlier days, a shoe maker's shop and then a gun smith; now it was a comfortable old bar with Cubs' pennants on the wall and sports posters of some of the great boxers of the time like Jack Dempsey, Joe Louis and Rocky Marciano. Eddie had a pair of boxing gloves hanging up behind the bar that he said belonged to the great Jack Dempsey and wouldn't let anybody touch them.

Plenty of tables on the main floor meant lots of people. Everyone liked coming to Eddie's. Upstairs there were pool tables, card tables and dart boards if you wanted to play but mostly people just came to Eddie's to hang out and relax.

Lou walked in at about 7:00 PM and sat down in his usual spot at the end of the bar, away from people, and just looked around.

The place had a few regulars sitting around and nothing seemed to be out of the norm. With his first cold one in front of him, Lou settled in for the evening.

Chapter 3

Nothing ruins a man's routine more than questions early in the morning. Lou wasn't looking for company but here it was.

On his way down the street to get his morning paper, Andy Ames stepped out of his barbershop and sat on the stoop. "Hey Lou!" he said. "Did you hear Geno's got broken into last night? He got roughed up pretty bad, his wife too. I hear they won big at the track yesterday and word must have gotten around. The police are still at his place, but Geno is in the hospital and his wife is a mess."

Lou continued on to Benny's newsstand and picked up his papers while Benny filled him in as much as he could. "Word has it two guys b-broke into the b-b back of the shop and went upstairs at about 10:00 PM. M-most likely they were after the m-m-money Geno's wife won at the track. People are saying Geno f-fought them off p-pretty good but they c-cold c-c-cocked him and roughed him up b bad and his wife too. They got the m-money, Lou."

He walked away from the newsstand, always amazed at just how much information Benny had about the street and the people that lived there.

Back in his room Lou tried to start his routine like always but as he sat by his window trying to read the want ads he thought of Geno and his wife and what they had just gone through for a few bucks. He told himself he would ask around and maybe catch a break. It was the least he could do, Geno was a friend.

The want ads were full of shit jobs: waiters, salesmen, dockworkers and factory workers, all of which Lou wanted nothing to do with. If anyone asked how it was going, at least he could say he was trying.

He was making for the track and his hotdog, but stopped at Geno's Bakery on the way. The store was closed and there was a big policeman standing guard at the front door, swinging his Billy Club in ways that were pretty impressive. "Move along sir," the policeman said, "nothing to see here."

Lou looked up from under his hat and a big smile came to his face. "I swear Shamus, you're getting uglier every day," he poked. "This is what they got you doing now you old Irishman?"

The policeman hadn't recognized Lou right away and was about to thump him with his stick, but his eyes lit up as he recognized his old friend of many years. "I thought you were dead Grimes!" Shamus laughed.

Shamus was tall, around 6'5, barrel-chested, with a little extra weight these days since he had been on the force for nearly 34 years. He had short, curly brown hair and an easy smile for his friends.

"Where have you been? I heard they busted you back to rookie and had you guarding a lunch counter at a grade school," Lou howled back at him.

The two shook hands and swore that it had been too long and they had to get together over a beer to catch up. Lou said that he was headed to Saul's for a hotdog and Shamus's mouth began to water as he remembered Saul Gronski's hotdogs.

Shamus told Lou that he would be at the shop for a few more hours and maybe head over to the track for lunch. He told Lou what had happened at Geno's and that the place was locked up, waiting for a detective to arrive. Lou asked if he could look around the outside of the building for a minute and Shamus didn't see the harm, besides Lou was an ex-police detective for Christ sake!

True to his word, he just walked around the building looking for anything out of the ordinary in the alleyway. The backdoor was indeed smashed in and now sported a brand new piece of plywood where a door had been. It had rained during the night and the alleyway was water and mud and not much else.

Lou could see where the men had kicked the door in. He could tell they had to have been big men because of their foot prints in the mud and one had a split in the heel of a large left shoe. He could also see where a car had been parked because there was fresh oil on the ground and footprints leading to the back door. While making mental notes, Lou couldn't help but wish he had something to write on.

He walked back to the street and up to Shamus, he reminded his friend about getting together for a beer soon, maybe over at Eddie's. He asked Shamus for a piece of paper to make a note. With that done, he stuffed the paper in his pocket and walked away.

As always, Saul's hotdogs were little pieces of heaven all wrapped up in a steamy bun, with a bit of yellow gold to top it off. While Saul dished out Lou's meal, he asked him if he had heard anything about the break-in at Geno's. Saul said that everyone had heard about it but he couldn't help Lou get any closer to Geno's attackers. He promised to let

Lou know as soon as he had heard anything, but for now they would have to wait.

Lou went up to Stella's window and placed the most ridiculous bet she had ever heard and was about to give him hell when he stopped her and told her about Geno and his wife. Stella became very upset. She knew the baker and his wife very well and was pleased for them when their horse came in.

"How much did they win Stella?" Lou probed. Though she wasn't allowed to give this information out, this time was different.

"$500 Lou, I've never seen two people happier. I hate it when things like this happen," she said. "Are you going to look into it?" she asked.

"Just asking a couple of questions, doll. Do you have a piece of paper?"

Before she could hand him one, he wrote on his betting slip. He then walked out to the track to not only watch his horse lose, but he didn't even get out of the starting gate!

He was about to rip up the stub and throw it away, but remembered he had written on it and would need it later. He walked by Stella's window to the front doors, but she called to him and waved him over.

"Lou," she said looking stressed. "I remembered something about yesterday I think you should know. When I gave Geno the $500, they were both cheering loudly and waving the money in the air. I didn't think of it as being a bad thing at the time, but as they left the track I noticed two shady looking characters following pretty close behind them. Both were tall and heavy-set. One had a beard and the other no hair at all I think. They kept their heads down and their hands in their pockets as they made their way to the doors."

Lou watched Stella as she told him what she saw and noted that she was upset and still able to recall the events of yesterday with good detail. "Thanks doll," he said. "That's a great help. I need another piece of paper to get all this down."

Before he left he told her to try and relax and he would ask around to see what turned up. He made his way to the door and she watched him leave and thought to herself. "He's on this now, he might not know it yet, but he will."

Two days later Geno was released from the hospital and was resting at home in his bed over top of the bakery. Geno's wife, Marianne was in the shop when Lou came through the front door.

The bell on the door that announced customers startled her reminding her she wasn't fully recovered from the ordeal of a few nights ago. She still showed signs of being mugged with bruising on her face and arms, but she came up to Lou and put her arms around him and began to sob.

"It's good to see you Lou," she cried, "I guess you heard what happened."

He nodded his head slowly and gave her another hug. "Is there anything I can do for you Marianne?" he said in a low voice.

"I'll be fine Lou, but you should talk to Geno," she replied. "He's angry as hell and won't rest, says he's going to kill the guys that did this to us as soon as he recovers. His pride is hurt Lou. They came into our home and he was unable to protect us. He's scaring me, never seen him this way before."

Lou told her he'd have a word with Geno and went up the back stairs to their living quarters. Geno was lying on the bed, bruised and swollen with a bandage over his head and one eye closed. He didn't see Lou right away and grabbed for his baseball bat when he heard a noise.

"Hold up there Geno, it's me, Lou Grimes. I came over to see if you need any help while you heal up."

Geno released the bat and sat back. "Thanks Lou, but we'll be ok."

"Can you describe them to me Geno? Had you ever seen them before?" Lou probed.

"Never seen these guys before Lou, but when I do, I'll kill them like the dogs they are."

Lou sat back and let Geno talk. "There were two of them, tall, very tall. One had a beard and the other was bald. Both wore long car coats and work pants and didn't waste any time with small talk. They wanted the money we won at the track and they were going to have it. They beat me down with a pipe and began working on Marianne when I finally gave in and told them where to look. The bald man was the most nervous and asked his partner, Frank if he found the cash."

"The bearded man's name was Frank?" Lou sat up.

"Yeah, but that was all that was said. Then they left out the back door and drove away."

Lou started making notes on a corner of a newspaper that was on Geno's bedside.

"You lookin into this Lou?" Geno asked. "Are you on the case?"

"Just asking a couple of questions old friend, relax now." Lou said as he stuffed the piece of newspaper in his pocket with the rest of his notes. With that he was out the door heading for Eddie's.

Chapter 4

A week had gone by with no word from the police about Geno's mugging and robbery. He did invite Shamus over to Eddie's for beers to catch up but it was also to pick his friend's brain as to how things were progressing.

Lou had given him what information he had about the shoe prints, the two suspects' description and the fact that one of them was named Frank and the word had gone out around the neighborhood to keep their eyes and ears perked.

Shamus was impressed, but told Lou to stay out of it, he was a civilian now and to let the police do their job.

Tuesday night came around, like it did every week. It was poker night and Lou and his buddies found themselves around a poker table at Eddie's, telling tall tales, drinking beer and trying to make a few bucks.

Shamus had been invited and fit right in with the rogues' gallery around the table. There was Lou, Eddie,

Tommy D, a local trucker and ladies' man and Archie Holmes who drove a milk truck and now the newest member, Shamus.

Other than Shamus, the guys had known each other for quite some time so it was hard to bluff your hand. Lou was up a dollar or two, Eddie around five, Shamus was losing and so was Tommy D.

Lou could tell that something was bothering Archie. He didn't seem to be following what was going on and wasn't talking very much. When the game broke up, Lou took Archie aside and asked him what the problem was.

Archie took a deep breath and out it came. "It's my wife Lois, Lou. I think she's cheating on me, but I can't prove it. I'm on the truck early in the morning and loading it at night."

Archie looked at Lou; his eyes widened and he grabbed his shirt. "You used to be a cop, Lou." Archie's voice was getting louder. "You would know about how to find out stuff like this and get something on her if she was sleeping around. It's driving me nuts Lou," he said. "I gotta know."

Lou put his hands on Archie's shoulders and told him that he wasn't a cop anymore, just a private citizen. Archie became upset. "Just follow her around quiet like for a day or so, just to see what she does. I'll pay you fifty bucks for two day's work Lou, even if you don't find anything."

This was something Lou knew how to do and he could use the cash. Against his better judgment, Lou nodded. "Okay Archie, two days and then I walk away," he heard himself saying.

Archie gave Lou his address and delivery schedule as he left the bar muttering to himself. "I got you now you bitch."

Early the next morning, Lou was sitting in Eddie's 1935 Ford Model 48, just down the street from Archie's apartment as he left for work. He figured it would be an easy fifty because he didn't believe Lois was stepping out.

He stayed out there the entire day and evening until Archie came home. "Twenty-five dollars in his pocket and twenty-five to go," he thought. "He needed a piss, a hamburger sandwich and a beer in that order, all available at Eddie's!"

His favorite bartender had started the sandwich service some time back and it was going over in a big way. Eddie had turned an old back room into a kitchen of sorts where he now had help for the lunch and evening crowd. Eddie felt he didn't want to lose the business of patrons having to leave his establishment when they got hungry. It was simple fare, mainly sandwiches and on weekends the cook would indulge in a passable Irish stew.

Eddie's part-time help came in the form of Terry O'Doyle. He was a part-time barman, dishwasher, sandwich maker and when needed, bouncer but mostly Terry O'Doyle was Eddie's friend.

They grew up together and survived on the streets of Chicago by having each other's backs when it was needed. Terry was a good ten inches taller than Eddie and the tougher of the two.

In his early years rather than going to school like Eddie, he wanted to be a boxer and fought in the rings and bare-knuckle contests for money around the city. As good as he thought he was others were much better.

Terry took too many right fists to his face and many beatings to his body. Eventually it affected his health and he was told to retire or die. He had nothing to fall back on and eventually found himself on the streets, homeless and penniless.

Eddie had found him on Barnaby's Row in a soup kitchen line and offered him a job at the bar and a place to live. It was a friendship renewed and Terry would defend Eddie to the death.

Lou was finishing his sandwich on his first stakeout night when a thought came to him. "What proof? How was he going to get it? He needed a picture!"

He knew that Eddie's uncle owned a photography parlor next to Lenny's Smoke Shop and he asked Eddie if he thought he could borrow a camera. Eddie made a phone call and made arrangements to borrow a camera for the next day. Lou had to promise Eddie to have it back the next day in one piece and pay his bar tab when he got paid.

This sounded like a winning proposition to Lou, so off he went early the next morning to wait the day out and collect his pay.

The morning was a breeze. Lou had made himself a peanut butter sandwich to take along and brought a beer as well. It was a warm beer, but a beer just the same.

Archie came back for lunch and was out the door in under a half an hour.

Lou could see the finish line now, but no such luck. Archie wasn't gone more than an hour when up to the apartment building rolls this 1927 Ford Model T, or Jitney as it was known. Lois came bouncing out the door to jump into the car and plant a big wet kiss on the oily bastard with a pencil thin moustache.

"Alright you little bitch, let's play," Lou said to himself.

The couple drove away, totally unaware that a car was following them about a half a block back. They drove down to the industrial part of town and got a room in a nasty little shithole called "The Bird of Paradise."

Lou waited for them to go inside before taking a picture of the outside of the motel. It seemed to be a good idea. Twenty minutes later he kicked in the motel door and the flash bulb went off and Lou got his money shot! Lois and Mr. Oily were caught in a very compromising position and it only got better as the naked couple tried to escape the flashbulbs by running into the bathroom with everything hanging out!

Lou gathered up Mr. Oily's pants which contained his wallet and car keys and Lois' dress and undergarments. "Here's your proof, Archie," he mumbled under his breath.

All Lou heard from behind the bathroom door as he was leaving the room was "who the hell was that?" and "well, we're in the shit now, Lloyd."

Lou laughed his ass off all the way back to Eddie's. It was only 6:00 o'clock and he had plenty of time to have one of those famous hamburger sandwiches and a beer before meeting Archie after he got off from work.

He was on his third beer when Archie came into the bar and walked right up to Grimes. "Well?" he asked.

"The money first," Lou replied.

Archie paid his friend what he owed and Lou handed over the bag containing the clothing.

Archie looked at the bag and asked "what's this?"

"Christmas present buddy. You can open it now, or wait for the pictures," Lou said and turned back to his beer.

"Son of a bitch," Lou heard Archie hiss as he turned and walked out of the bar.

Eddie was standing back behind the bar, casually cleaning a beer glass, but was listening to what was going on, which he always did.

With Archie gone, Eddie slowly sauntered up to his friend, still looking down, wiping the glass. "That was good work Lou. You've still got it," he said. "Now pay your bar tab!"

Chapter 5

Back in his room, Lou lay on his bed in the dark, unable to sleep. He watched the blinking streetlights make shadows on his wall.

He had done a good thing today; he helped a friend but it brought back bitter memories of the night he found Trixie in bed with Ralph. He remembered how she had hurt him to his core by calling him less of a man than her lover and threw the alarm clock at him as he left.

For the next couple of days life went back to normal for Lou and his routine. He still ate hotdogs at Saul's, still caught hell from Stella about his pony choices, still had meals at Maude's and of course still frequented his stool at Eddie's.

On Tuesday night the guys found themselves around the card table again, minus one. Shamus, still new to the group, asked the obvious question "what's happened to Archie tonight? I wanted to take his money again."

"Archie found out his wife was cheating on him," Eddie said. "When he confronted her about it, she threw his stuff out in the hall of their apartment and locked him out, vowing to call the police if he didn't leave."

"Holy shit, guys, really?" Shamus said, wide-eyed.

Tommy D added to the conversation by saying that Archie had found a rooming house down on Front Street and was "dealing with it." "He told me not to say anything, but it will get around soon enough."

"Christ guys that must have been hard for him to deal with. How did he find out?" Shamus was curious now and would not let it go.

Lou finally broke his silence. "Archie paid me to follow Lois for two days just to see if what he was thinking was true. I tracked her and her boyfriend to a sleazy motel down by the industrial area, kicked the door in and took a few Christmas card snapshots and a few mementos. Archie paid me fifty bucks, took the shit I found there and that was the last I saw of him."

Shamus put his elbows on the table and his chin in his closed hands, leaned forward and looked at Lou. "You do realize that you're not a cop anymore," he began. "What you did was dangerous and against the law. This guy, Lois's bed buddy, what if he had a gun when you broke into the room?

You would have looked real stupid lying there dead in the middle of a sleazy motel room. The papers would make a field day out of it. Headlines would read 'EX-COP FOUND DEAD.' Besides, the motel owner could have charged you for kicking in his door and scaring off a paying customer. There will be no more of that nonsense Mr. Grimes, is that clear? Find a real job!"

Lou hadn't thought of it that way. It made sense. He reached over the table and shook Shamus' hand. "Okay Officer, I promise."

Chapter 6

The weather in Chicago, for October, was pretty decent. The average temperatures were between 54 and 63 degrees, jacket weather really, if you didn't mind the wind.

Chicago was a melting pot of anticipation and excitement. It was hot enough to make you sweat if you were a Cubs fan. The World Series was in town because Chicago had won the National League Pennant with a record of 98 to 56, three games ahead of St. Louis.

It'd been 37 years since the Cubs had last won the series and the entire city was wrapped up in World Series fever. The Cubs were playing an old rival, the Detroit Tigers and Lou was planning on spending the week the series was in town on his seat at Eddie's bar, listening to the games on the radio.

He was a huge Cubs fan and had been his entire life. He had been at Weeghman Park in 1914, the day it opened and there again in 1926 when the park was renamed "Wrigley Field."

Lou woke on Wednesday morning with a plan for the next week, baseball. Today was the start of the World Series and he was determined to listen to it all. The horse he was going to bet on today was even called "Major League." "How could he lose?" he thought. But he did.

Not to be deterred, Lou walked into Eddie's that afternoon, ordered a beer and a sandwich and listened to the series opener. His Cubs defeated the Tigers 9 to 0. It turned out to be a great day after all!

Over the next two days, the game wins went back and forth. By the day of game four, the Cubs were ahead, two games to one. Lou was in his favorite spot and the place was full of customers listening.

The announcer was situated just outside the stadium talking to crowds of people coming through the gate when a commotion started up at one of the turnstiles. A man was trying to bring a goat into the stadium and was being denied.

Crowds were gathering around the man and were complaining that the goat smelled bad and he should take it away. The man said the goat was his pet named "Murphy" and didn't smell that bad once you got used to it.

Finally the owner of the goat, William Sianis, who owned the Billy Goat Tavern agreed to tie the goat up outside but the crowd and security, said that that wasn't going to happen either and he was turned away.

The man was so enraged that as he was leaving the stadium he shouted out to the crowd and waved his fists. "Them Cubs, they ain't gonna win no more!" He then walked away.

The announcer came back on the radio and stated that it sounded like an angry fan had just put a curse on the Cubs baseball team.

Maybe the curse worked. The Cubs lost the game 4 to 1. The goat thing was the talk of Eddie's bar the rest of the day and into the night.

Shamus came into the bar around 9:00 o'clock that evening and ordered a beer and a sandwich.

Lou looked over at him and asked "where have you been you old devil?"

Shamus stretched and rubbed his tired muscles. "Working at the game today, lots of people drinking lots of beer makes a long day. There was even a guy there trying to get his pet goat into the stadium. It caused quite a stink, if you know what I mean," he said with a chuckle.

Lou said that he had been listening and that the announcer said it sounded like some nut job put a curse on the team. "According to him they would never win a championship again."

"Nonsense," Shamus said as he drank his beer, "just a nut."

Shamus then turned to Lou and put a big smile on his face. Lou saw the shit-eating grin and replied. "You've got a secret, don't you, you big Irish Mick."

"I do my friend, I do," Shamus came back. "How would you like to go to game six with me? I'm working that game and you can get in with me. That is, if you're not too busy looking for a job or saving some old lady's cat from a tree."

Lou near fell off the stool! A dream was coming true. "I don't know what to say my friend, the least I can do is buy you another beer."

Monday rolled in and Lou took a trolley to Wrigley Field, early like Shamus had asked him, so as to clear him in as his guest.

Shamus hadn't gotten him a great seat, it was out in left field half way up the bleachers, but it was his seat and he was at the World Series, Game Six, 1945!

Lou knew every statistic there was about his baseball team and even had a favorite pitcher, Paul Derringer. According to Lou, Derringer's curve ball was the best in the league and his fast ball was like lightening being released from his hand.

It was a great game and Lou lived every moment of it. They even went into overtime with the Cubs winning 8 to 7 in the 12th inning. The Series was now tied, 3 to 3.

He was on cloud 9 as he stepped off the trolley and went into Eddie's doing a victory dance up to the bar. This was the year, he could feel it.

Tuesday's card game was full of excitement and anticipation of game seven the next day. Archie was there and everybody vowed to be at the bar to listen to the game and cheer on the Cubs to victory!

The next day everyone was around a table at Eddie's with a Cubs' pennant in the middle of it. They listened to their team go down in defeat to the Tigers, 9 to 3! To Lou it was like someone had punched him in the gut as he thought to himself, "was the curse of the Billy Goat for real?"

He was sure the rest of the city was in mourning the next day, but life has to go on and "we'll win next year!"

He walked down the street to get his paper and racing forms, and people were stopping him, saying what a great series it was and how "we were robbed."

Benny told him that the headlines in the papers were awful and that it was best if Lou didn't read them.

Back in his room he made strong coffee and was determined to find a job, maybe.

Everything he read made him angry. "Be your own boss," he read. "Door to door sales, was a job for the future!"

He threw the newspaper across the room and looked closer at his racing form. "Hard Luck Sally" in the fourth was at 25 to 1. "Why not," he thought.

Saul's was an island in the storm of life. The hotdog was incredible as always and Saul mentioned that Shamus had stopped by earlier and wanted to meet Lou at Maude's for coffee at around 3 that afternoon and that another small shop had been robbed over on 6th Street and they got away clean.

"Hard Luck Sally" was exactly that and Lou went away with a feeling that the whole world was against him. The day got even worse on the way to Maude's as one of the neighbors had left their damn door open and a big dog got out and grabbed Lou by the pant leg as he was walking by and wouldn't let go. "Christ," he said to himself, "could this day get any shittier?"

The rest of his walk was uneventful, which was a good thing because Lou's disposition had worsened and he was not in a good mood. He headed straight to Maude's. He needed a coffee and a sandwich and most of all a piss. "Must be getting old," he thought, "always seem to be in the John these days."

Maude had set him up nicely with coffee and a paper and was in the process of making him a huge roast beef sandwich when Shamus came through the door. "You're early," he said as he came up and sat across from Lou, smiling.

"I cleared my afternoon calendar just for you, buddy," Lou said sarcastically, still grumpy.

Shamus wasn't interested in Lou's little pity party and got right to the point. "It's time you got off your ass and got back to doing what you do," he said.

Lou looked up at him and gave him a snappy comeback. "In case you haven't noticed, and it's something you like to remind me of a lot, I'm not a detective anymore."

"Doesn't mean you can't do the job though," Shamus came back quickly.

"What the hell do you mean?" Lou was in no mood for riddles.

Shamus was just as quick with the comeback lines as Lou was. "Private Detective," he said flatly. "You could be a Private Detective. You've got all the skills. People trust you and come to you for help. Why not get paid for it?"

"That's insane Shamus," Lou said. "Who the hell is going to hire me?"

"People already are," Shamus replied, "and you're making money at it. This time though, it would be legal. I can throw you a little work from time to time. It's skip-chasing, but the money is good and you know what the work is. Find the bad guy, bring them back to the law and get paid. You've done that many times before as a real cop, for less money. What do you say Lou? Are you in?"

Chapter 7

The next morning Lou was at City Hall writing his Private Investigator's exam and paying his $20 to the clerk. Hours later Lou Grimes was sitting on his favorite stool in his favorite bar looking down at a Private Investigator's License and a brand new, shiny badge.

He had been there awhile, looking down at his new future when Eddie came over to him and noticed what he was looking at. "You back on the job Lou?" his friend smiled.

"Kind of Eddie, gonna try the private side of the law for awhile, see if it fits," he replied.

"Well I'll be damned," Eddie mumbled as he moved away.

The phone in Eddie's bar, located on the wall between a doorway leading to a small storage room and the men's washroom rang. Eddie moved to answer the phone and talked for a minute before calling over to Lou "it's for you Dick Tracy," he said jokingly, "and I ain't your secretary."

Lou made his way over to the phone and grabbed the hanging receiver. "Hello?" he said. It turned out to be Shamus and after finding out that Lou had indeed got his license, he congratulated him. He told Lou that he would pick him up on Monday morning and take him downtown to talk to Abe. All Lou could say was, "thank you, and who the hell's Abe?"

Lou didn't know it at the time, but he was about to be introduced to Abraham Schwarz, the sole owner and operator of Schwarz and Son Bail Bond Inc., established in 1910 and one of the shrewdest bondsmen in the city of Chicago.

Abraham, Abe to his friends, was a true Orthodox Jew in every sense of the word; from his long curly sideburns and straight beard to his black, flat-brimmed hat and black attire, Abraham was as devout to his religion as he was to money.

He was short, thin, and in his 50's with tiny wire rimmed glasses that hung from his nose. Abe was all business.

His office was located in the heart of Chicago near the Police Station. Abe would often tell his friends "it's a prime location and good for business."

It was just another two-storey walk up as were most of the buildings in the area. Abe's office faced the street with another smaller room in the back. Abe and his wife Ruth lived upstairs.

Abraham was always telling people that would listen that Ruth kept him fed and did the books. Ruth was built-in cheap labor.

Abraham's workspace consisted of one small old desk with a gooseneck lamp on it, two chairs, three overly filled filing cabinets with more stacks of files and papers on top of them. A phone, a calendar on the wall and coat tree completed the room. The thing that was really noticeable was the heavy smell of Abraham's pipe tobacco that seemed to hang on everything.

The painted sign on the window said "Schwarz and Son" but Abraham had no sons. He said it sounded better and was good for business.

Shamus and Lou came around Abe's bail bond shop at about 9:30 Monday morning. Shamus and Abraham went way back so when Shamus told him he had a new P.I. with over 25 years' experience as a policeman, he listened.

Lou and Abraham hit it off right away. It was like they had known each other for years. Lou was looking for work and Abe had files that needed to be closed, fast.

After half an hour of conversation, Abraham stood up and shook Lou's hand and said "Okay, I'll give you a try."

Abraham took a file off the top of many others and gave it to Lou. "This lowlife beat his wife up after a weekend of partying. She had him arrested and thrown in jail, and also filed a restraining order for him to stay away when he got out.

"The Judge set his bail at $5,000 and he came to me to make his bail and used his house as collateral. He missed his scheduled appearance last week and that means I'll be out $500 and on the hook for $4,500 more if you can't find him and turn him over to the cops, quick. The court doesn't give you much time."

Lou said he'd be in touch and left with Shamus to go back to his office and study the file. It was Monday afternoon and he would have to work fast.

He sat on his stool and studied the material in the file. He had seen this stuff many times before when he was a cop. There was an arrest report, name and address, a copy of the collateral in trust, and the restraining order.

Lou read on,

"Sean O'Leary, white male, 39, arrested before for drunk and disorderly, lived at 4219 Green Street East in Rockview, a suburb in East Chicago."

This was a middle income, family area.

The report also said he was a driver at "City Trucking," making deliveries in the greater Chicago area.

Before Lou could start on the file he had to address his first concern and that was transportation. He convinced Eddie to rent his car to him for $2 a day and he would take care of the fuel. That done, he had lunch at Maude's and was on his way over to the O'Leary address just on the off chance Sean had showed up there.

No such luck. His wife Linda was a real mess. He had beaten her pretty badly and Lou was sure she was missing a couple of teeth. The place was not in good shape either with broken chairs and lamps and kids running around getting into everything.

Linda had three kids that had not been in the report. She looked tired, really tired and had not wanted to cause so much trouble. However, she got fire hot when Lou told her that Sean had skipped his court appearance and was nowhere to be found. Worse yet, he had used the house as collateral.

If they didn't find him, the house would be sold out from under her and she and the kids would be out on the street.

She was fit to be tied and screamed at the top of her lungs. She told Lou about Sean's work and his hangouts and where he liked to drink and as he turned and headed down the stairway, she yelled at him from the doorway "don't forget that slut girlfriend of his! He might be with her. I know he's sleeping around, he stinks of cheap perfume when he comes home late and only tells me what he thinks I need to know."

With this new information, Lou headed back to Eddie's to go over what he had just learned. Tomorrow was another day.

Seeing that it was a weekday, Lou headed over to Sean's place of employment. City Trucking was located down near the warehousing part of town. The place turned out to be a wealth of information for the new gumshoe. It seemed that Sean wasn't well liked by other employees. He had not been into work in over a week and had been let go because of it.

As Lou was getting back in the car, a truck driver came up to him and told him that Sean had been pretty "cozy" with a secretary that used to work there, but didn't any more. Her name was Charlotte something or other. Lou needed more information and went back into the office and charmed the new secretary into giving him Charlotte's address.

He found the address easy enough. Now it was just a matter of time and a little patience to see if his hunch was correct. He sat in the car watching her apartment from just down the street for the better part of that day and into the night.

Sure enough, around 11:30 PM Lou saw a man walking unsteadily down the sidewalk with a bottle in his hand. The man stopped at the address and tried to fish a key out of his pocket with no success.

Lou's senses came alive and his hunch was paying off. He got out of the car and walked up the street, stopping at the apartment. He asked the guy if he needed any help. "Can't find my damn key," Sean's voice was slurred.

"Maybe it's because you're at the wrong address, Sean. Don't you live at 4219 Green Street in Rockview?" Lou said quietly.

Sean was quicker than Lou had thought he would be and was out of his reach and running down the street before he could react.

The thrill of the chase came back to him quickly and he remembered how much he loved it. Sean was getting away from him and turned down an alley about 50 feet ahead. That was his mistake. The alley had no exit and he was trapped and ready to fight.

Lou turned into the alley and Sean was on him from out of nowhere. He side-stepped Sean's first and only punch as his old "blackjack" slid into his hand and came slamming down on Sean's head, crumpling him to the ground.

Two minutes later Sean came around to find his hands cuffed behind his back, and sitting in the dirt.

He never shut up all the way back to the Police Station about what kind of asshole Lou was and what he was going to do to him when he got out.

"Keep chirping chump," Lou smiled, "I'm not hard to find."

Lou drove up to the Police Station and walked Sean through the front door and up to the desk. He knew the Sergeant working there from before and smiled "Terry?"

The Sergeant looked up and a big grin came over his face. "Lou Grimes," he said, "where have you been and what's that you've got there?"

"Something you lost, Terry my man. I'm returning it," he responded.

Lou filled out some paperwork, made sure he had a copy and left, listening to Sean protest as they dragged him back to the cells.

It had been a good day for Lou Grimes. He was back doing what he loved to do and tomorrow he'd have some cash too.

He stopped at Eddie's for a quick beer and then off to his room to have the best night's sleep he'd had in quite some time.

Chapter 8

Lou was up at 7:30. He could see his routine changing a little from now on, but for the most part, not much.

He walked down to the corner newsstand to get his racing form and say hello to Benny. He hadn't been there in a couple of days and wanted to catch up.

Firstly, Benny was happy to know that Lou was working again and promised to let him know if anything was out of place around the neighborhood. Once again, he told Lou about the activity around the old warehouse two blocks down.

Lou didn't think too much of it at the time. "That's swell Benny," Lou said. "Keep your eyes open kid and don't get into trouble."

He was going to head over to Abraham's around noon to get paid and see if there was any more work. He was sure there would be. Coffee at Maude's and his winner picked, "Touch of Class," Lou headed down to the track to place his $5 bet, get beat on by Stella and watch his long-shot come in fourth. He walked back to Eddie's, picked up the car and headed over to Abraham's.

A small bell chimed as he entered and Abe came out of the back room. Lou gave him his paperwork from the Police Station and Abe nodded his head and smiled. "You did well Mr. Grimes," and handed Lou an envelope. "There's $100 in there, that's 25% of the bail set and concludes our business for now."

Lou took the money and thanked Abe and asked if there were any other skips out there he could look for. "It's good to see that you are interested in continuing, Mr. Grimes. I always have files to close."

Abraham took another folder off the stack that was on his desk and handed it to Lou. "This one's more serious, the stakes are higher and so is the money if you bring him in."

He took the folder and said that he'd keep in touch. He left the office to settle in and study the file over a beer and sandwich at Eddie's.

He paid his bar tab and the rental fee on Eddie's car and still had more money in his pocket than he'd had in some time. It was a good feeling.

Eddie's was getting crowded and noisy so Lou walked up the street to Maude's. It would be quieter there and he could look closer at the file and his new runner.

He laid everything out on the table and Maude brought him a cup of coffee and patted him on the shoulder. "Good to see you back on the job Lou," she said.

He started reading the file. The man's name was Mickey Duluka.

"white male, 35, born 1910 in New York; no known address; tended to hang around pool halls on the south side; lived part time in the tramp camps down by the railroad under a train bridge; currently wanted for hijacking, grand theft auto, possession of stolen property over $10,000, driving without a license and a broken taillight."

He had a list of priors that read:

"petty theft, pick pocketing, possession of stolen property, drunk and disorderly, and vagrancy."

Lou read the file and scratched his head wondering how this small time Schmo got this far in over his head and how could this loser come up with bail set at $50,000, or even 10 percent of that. "Hell," Lou thought, "he probably wouldn't be able to find 5,000 pennies if his life depended on it."

It just didn't make sense to the new gumshoe, so he read Mickey's statement:

> "I had been walking out of an alley on Front Street around 11:00 PM, heading to the rail yard with a half bottle of Double Thunder Whiskey that I had taken off a drunk I had come across sitting on the sidewalk, passed out. When I came out of the dark into the light of an old diner, I noticed a truck parked to the side with no driver in it. I looked around and saw a man in the diner and thought it must be the driver and he didn't appear to be watching the truck.
>
> "I checked the door to the truck and found that it was unlocked so I climbed inside to look around for something I could take and sell. There was nothing that I could see.
>
> "I sat there wondering what was in the back of the truck, when I noticed the steering wheel cover was missing and the wires were bare. If I had learned anything during my misspent youth, it was that I could hot wire a vehicle.
>
> "I was thinking about a million things at one time but one thing was crystal clear. If I could get it started, I was going to steal this truck.

"I stripped the lead wires and twisted them together in order to use the starter button on the floor. I got the engine started, hit the gas pedal and roared out of the driveway and into the night.

"I was heading to the harbor to hide and look at what I was carrying when I ran a red light in front of a parked cruiser. I tried to outrun the cruiser but was pulled over five miles later when two police cars caught up to me and ran me into a ditch."

The report went on further to state:

"After I was arrested and put in the back of the cruiser, the Police checked the back of the truck and found it full of boxes of bootleg whiskey and gin."

Mickey ended his statement by claiming he had no idea the truck was full of bootleg booze, or how it got there.

Lou sat there shaking his head when his old friend and poker player, Police Sergeant Shamus O'Hearn came through the door of the Diner. "Maude," he yelled, "what's the special?"

He came over to where Lou was sitting and slammed his ass down in the booth, "haven't seen you in a couple of days Lou, by the way, congrats on the collar. The guy was an asshole and deserves what he gets. Abe says he liked the way you handled yourself and gave you another file."

Lou just nodded. "Which one did you draw?" Shamus asked. Lou gave him the arrest sheet and waited for him to finish reading it. "You drew the joker on this one Lou. He's been on the run for over a week now and it's only a matter of time before we pull his dead body from the east river tied to a couple of cement blocks. Word on the street was that that booze truck he boosted belonged to Tommy "Big Nose" Danza, and you know who he works for, don't you?"

Lou shook his head again and Shamus continued. "Paul Ricca is the Crime Syndicate's current boss of bosses, directly picked by Capone himself to succeed him. That is bad news for Mickey Duluka. Paul Ricca will stop at nothing to get his hands on Duluka, make an example of him and get his booze back."

"How the hell did this nothing of a bum get his hands on $50,000?" Lou sighed and sat back. His head was beginning to hurt.

A lot had happened to Mickey during that short time. Lou could only imagine.

Chapter 9

Kevin Heller had just finished up his supper at Joe's Diner and was going to have a piss before jumping back into his truck and deliver the last load of recently distilled hooch to Tommy's warehouse on Walker Street on the east side. This booze would be distributed to all the bars and dance halls that Paul Ricca controlled and they in turn would pay a premium price for his protection. This was just the way it was and nobody dared complain.

Kevin walked out into the driveway and his mouth fell open. The load was gone! The truck and its contents were not there.

If he had not gone to relieve himself he would have pissed himself right there, out of pure fear for his life. He broke into a cold sweat and his lips went dry. "Who would be stupid enough to jack Tommy "Big Nose" Danza's truck?" Now he had to do something that scared the hell out of him. He had to call the warehouse and tell them Tommy's booze had been stolen on his watch.

He went back into the diner and used the wall phone to make a call he thought he would never have to make. It rang and rang and rang again until a voice on the other end answered. "Yeah, what do you want?"

Kevin wet his lips before answering. "Somebody has boosted the booze. I swear it wasn't me," Kevin pleaded.

"Where are you now?" the voice asked.

"Joe's Diner, down by the waterfront," he answered.

"Stay put," the voice said. "I'll have someone pick you up." Then he hung up.

Calls were made to dangerous people and then Tommy Danza was finally told that his load was missing. Kevin Heller was never seen again.

Chapter 10

Tommy Danza would have to explain this loss to his boss, Paul Ricco at the next meeting in New York City, but by that time, the matter would be resolved and the guilty parties dealt with. An example would be made to show the public that Tommy "Big Nose" Danza and the Syndicate would not be made fools of.

The word went out immediately to the streets that the Syndicate was looking for its stolen property and a reward was offered.

Street people get arrested and the city holding centre was abuzz about the booze heist. This news finally got to Mickey Duluka's cell and he knew he was a dead man, but right now he was safe where he was. No one in lockup really knew why he was there but the cops did and the money offered as a reward would be substantial. It was only a matter of time before a call from the city lockup went to Tommy's people on the street that the police were holding a man for driving a stolen truck and that it was loaded with bootleg liquor.

"Thank you for your assistance" the voice on the other side of the receiver said. "You will of course be compensated. Leave the rest to us and we will clean up the mess. By the way," the voice said. "Where are they holding my truck?"

"West side Police Yards," the other voice stated. "I hope this helps."

"It will indeed," the other voice said, "goodbye."

The next call Tommy Danza made was to his fixer, named Pierce. "Get him out of there and get my truck back!"

Back at the Police Station, the silence on the phone was scary as hell, but Ralph didn't care. He had just made a pile of dough and all it cost him was a phone call.

Chapter 11

Abraham Schwarz was sitting at his old desk Tuesday morning, contemplating his day when the door chime activated and in walked a tall thin man with a very narrow face, beady little black eyes, pencil-thin mustache, and sporting a gold tooth you could see when he smiled and Abe noted he smiled a lot. He wore black, all black from his spats to his gloves. His briefcase was quality leather.

Abe glanced outside and saw a very large chauffeur standing next to a big black limousine. The visitor slid silently over to Abe's desk and put his briefcase out in front of him.

"Mr. Schwarz, my name is Charles Pierce and I'm here representing a relative of a Mr. Mickey Duluka who wishes to remain anonymous and post his bail.

Abe didn't need the introduction; this was Charlie, "Pinkie" Pierce, a very dangerous man and the lawyer for Tommy Danza and the Crime Syndicate Boss, Paul Ricca.

Before Abe could speak up, Charlie reached into his briefcase and pulled out five stacks of thousand dollar bills. "I believe the bail is set at $50,000. Is that correct?" he asked.

"That's right," Abe replied looking wide-eyed at the stacks of money, 10% to the courts and the remainder held as collateral."

"That's only fair," the lawyer answered as he turned and walked to the door.

"Oh Mr. Schwarz," he asked. "When will our poor Mickey be released so we can be sure to be there to pick him up?"

Abe was putting the money into his safe and answered without looking "should be early this afternoon, if the paperwork goes through without a hitch."

"See that it does, Mr. Schwarz, for your sake." Then he was gone.

Meanwhile, Mickey was sitting in his cell holding his head in his hands and worrying about his chances in here if the population found out that he was the one that hijacked the mob's booze. It wouldn't be good. Not good at all, he thought.

Lost in his thoughts, Mickey didn't see the guard come up to his window and peer in. "You're out of here this afternoon Duluka. Your cousin posted your bail."

Mickey's heart was racing a mile a minute, he didn't have a cousin and there was only one place that kind of dough could come from. The mob had found out where he was and now he was a dead man walking. "What was he going to do?" He knew they'd be waiting for him as soon as he left the building.

The guard walked Mickey to the front desk to complete his release papers and walked away. He completed the paperwork and was turning to the doorway when he saw his only hope, the fire alarm.

He moved quickly toward it on the wall and smashed the glass. He pulled the handle down and it set off a war zone of alarms so loud it was hard to think. He stood away from the door and waited for the masses of people in the building to run for their lives.

The mass panic arrived as promised and Mickey joined the crowd running out the door and slipped away down an alley.

Pierce and the two palookas were sitting in the limo, waiting for Mickey to show and were not prepared for the mass hysteria that came out of the front door and into the street. They had missed their prey this time but Duluka would be found and dealt with in short order.

Pierce would put the word out on the street that there was a contract out on Mickey Duluka and a large reward was offered to anyone that turned him in. It was only a matter of time.

Chapter 12

Lou sat in his booth at Maude's trying to think of his next move. He knew he didn't have much time and would have to move quickly or it would be too late. Mickey already had a big jump on him and could be out of town already or sitting at the bottom of the East River.

"What's your next move slick?" Shamus wanted to know.

"Don't have a clue, my friend," Lou said. "He has to eat and he has to sleep and he has to have a plan. I'll start with the flop houses and soup kitchens down by the harbor, then maybe drop into Hobo Town and ask around. You never know, I might get lucky. I still have a few sources on the street. Maybe one of them heard something."

The next morning early, Lou set off for an area in town called "Barnaby's Row." This was one of the many depressed areas in the city where people went to get lost or just survive. It was better known as "Skid Row."

Lou knew many of the people that inhabited the dark alleyways and narrow side streets here and he spent the better part of his day just walking around and talking to old friends and acquaintances, this was what being a gumshoe was about.

He visited the tattoo parlors, pool halls, whore houses, and soup kitchens that called the area home and asked the same question all the time. "Have you seen Mickey Duluka lately? Can you point me to someone who may have seen him?"

The street people knew Lou and trusted him, but they couldn't help. Near the end of the day, as Lou was walking back to his car, he passed a soup kitchen he had been in earlier. An old woman was now sitting on the stoop wearing an old dirty coat to protect her from the wind and the bite of an oncoming Chicago winter. Her name was Alice Skrantz.

She and Lou went way back to when he was a cop and had busted her for prostitution but let her go to be his eyes on the street.

He sat next to her on the stoop and offered her a cigarette and a swig of whiskey from a small flask he always carried. "It'll warm your insides, Alice," he smiled. She trusted Lou because he had given her a break awhile back and was a swell guy.

Lou just sat there and Alice offered information he found very interesting.

"Busy times on the street lately, Lou," she offered, "lots of questions being asked about your boy and where he might be. Lots of money being spread around too and men in black sedans shaking down flop houses laying on muscle, looking for him. He's not here Lou, I would know if he was."

Lou stood up and stretched his tired back and gave her a couple more cigarettes to thank her. He asked her to keep her eyes open and let him know if she heard anything. He then told her to try and stay warm and walked away.

Back at Eddie's that evening he came up with a plan to hit a lot of the churches in the area, just off Skid Row. It was a given these days that if you found a church, you'd find a soup kitchen in the back and if you found a soup kitchen, you'd find some caring old priest that would give you a place to sleep.

It took Lou the better part of the next day and into the evening to find what he was looking for, that caring old priest that couldn't say no to a scared, starving man with a story that could melt his heart.

Mickey had been there the last two days and had managed to convince the priest that he was an innocent victim and was being hunted for something he hadn't done.

He had told the priest that he was leaving town to stay alive and was heading for the Hobo Hilton to look for a way out.

The Hobo Hilton, Lou knew, was a place where transient people gathered under a train trestle a mile or so away from the church. People running away from something or just passing through would migrate to this place to wait, hop into an open boxcar and disappear into the night.

Lou knew that Mickey would be there by now so he had to move fast. If he had this information, so did his friends in the black sedans.

It took him fifteen minutes to get to the trestle and another ten minutes to find someone that would talk to him. The people that hung out there really didn't trust anyone who was asking questions.

He finally got a young man and his son, who were waiting to hop a car to New York, to talk to him.

The man said he had seen a desperate looking guy fifteen minutes prior, matching Lou's description of him. He had seen the man running into the rail yards looking to jump on anything that was moving out of the city and "Mr.," the young man said, "I don't think he was alone. Two real tough guys with guns were hot on his heals minutes later and they looked like they were all business."

Lou remembered that he didn't have a gun anymore, but he did have his blackjack and a piece of pipe he had picked up on his way into the rail yard. This and his wits was all he had and they would have to be enough.

He moved toward the rail yards where the young man had pointed and could see the two apes at the far side using their flashlights to look into the open railcars. They were making their way down the line and would eventually be right where Lou was standing. He crouched down in the dark and stayed still under a car then heard a noise to his right about twenty feet down the line of cars coming toward him making all kinds of racket. It was Mickey. He was falling down and getting up again and again in the loose rocks in his panic to escape the mob's hit men.

He didn't see Lou as he passed by him. Mickey was gasping for air and looking for better handholds so it was easy for Lou to step out behind him and hit him on the back of the head with his blackjack stunning him momentarily.

Mickey went to his knees and in that lapse of time Lou had cuffed him and was pulling him to his feet. He whispered into Mickey's ear "if you want to live for more than just a few more minutes, you better be quiet and come with me. If not, you're a dead man."

Mickey nodded and the two ran into the night and away from certain death.

They stepped out of the rail yard into the shadowy light of an old street lamp when the quiet was destroyed by the sound of gunfire from behind them and the shattering of a wooden pole next to Lou's face.

"We have to move fast and get into my car down the street. Don't stop for anything!"

More gunfire and Lou had his hat knocked off his head. The car was now only ten feet away when the gangsters came out of the yard, guns blazing in their direction. Suddenly there was silence. "They're reloading," Lou said as they both jumped into the car and sped away.

Gunfire erupted again and Eddie's car was the lucky recipient of two bullet holes in the back trunk and a broken side mirror. "Get down and stay down!" Lou yelled at Mickey.

Engines racing, tires squealing and guns were blazing into the night.

Lou tried to avoid being shot and to get to the Police Station with his prize in one piece.

He was zigzagging left and right and could see the Police Station just ahead of him but his hunters were just as close and were getting ready to ram them.

Lou hit the brakes hard and swerved to the left, sending the black sedan racing past and in front of them, losing control and smashing into a light standard in front of the Police Station.

The gunmen exited the sedan, guns blazing at Lou's car, only to be met by a larger hail of gunfire coming from the station house as policemen ran out, killing the gunmen where they stood.

More policemen came running out of the station, guns at the ready, but the fight was over. Only Lou and Mickey Duluka stood in the middle of the street among a dozen or so armed policemen and an old Desk Sergeant.

Terry Moans stood there scratching his head, wondering what the hell just happened until he saw Lou in the crowd. He walked up to his old friend and said, over all the commotion "this is your doing, isn't it Lou?"

"Yeah Terry, it is," he said. "But in my defence, you keep losing things and I have to go out there and find them." With that he handed over Mickey Duluka to two of Terry's Constables and walked into the Station. "You got any coffee worth drinking Terry?" he asked.

It was late by the time Lou got out of the Police Station. He finished the paperwork on Duluka and would see Abe in the morning. Right now, a cold beer or two was in order to calm his nerves and figure out a way to tell Eddie he got his car shot up.

Eddie took the news better than Lou expected, but he told his friend that he'd have to find his own set of wheels if he was going to continue being shot at.

Chapter 13

The next day Lou begged for the car one more time and drove to Abe's to hand in his paperwork and get paid.

Abraham was very impressed with his new bounty hunter and promised to make sure he would get all the work he could handle. For now, he was to take a few days off and unwind.

"I believe we agreed on 25%, if I'm not mistaken, and I rarely am," Abe mused. He handed Lou an envelope containing $1,250 and told him to get out of his office and have some fun.

Lou had not seen this type of dough in a very long time and had to think about it for awhile. He drove over to Maude's for breakfast and sat there in the booth for what seemed to be hours before coming up with a plan.

His plan came in three parts. Number one, he really liked what he was doing now, even if he was being shot at every now and then. Number two, he would get Eddie's car repaired. Number three, he was going to get his own car and let it be known around Chicago that he was "open for business."

Setting up Eddie's car repair was easy; every gas station had a mechanic/body-man on site. They were everywhere and would happily hammer out the holes and weld them shut. It was easy to find a replacement side mirror, so the $20 it cost in repairs was well spent.

Lou knew that he needed his own ride in order to do the job right, so before getting Eddie's car back to him, he drove around to a few used car dealerships to look around. He didn't want anything too fancy, but he didn't want a beast either. He wanted something in between, with a bit of power.

It took most of the afternoon but Lou finally decided on a used 1934 Hudson Terraplane KU Coupe. It was a six cylinder, two door with long flowing running boards and was black as night. To Lou, it was the best $200 he spent, and it was all his.

He drove Eddie's car back to him, thanked him and gave him another c-note just for being a friend.

Lou picked up his new ride the next morning and just drove around with no destination in mind. It was good to just not do anything like before, but this time, he had dough in his pocket to change things if he wanted to.

Word got around quickly that Lou was indeed "back on the job" in a private capacity and in the weeks to come started to get phone calls at Eddie's to take on all kinds of work. At the same time, Abraham Schwarz had files to close so Lou's services were in demand.

He still liked to play the ponies and the season was winding down. In a couple of weeks the tracks would close for the season and he'd have to place his bets in a parlor that catered to west coast racing.

Saul was in his usual spot and he congratulated Lou on making the right choice of work and told him to be careful where the mob was concerned. He had heard about the shootout in front of the Police Station.

Two hotdogs later and a big bag of roasted peanuts in hand, Lou went through the gates. He was sad the season would be ending soon, but for now, he still had time to make his fortune, chase bad guys and he had money in his pocket, so what the hell.

He hadn't seen Stella in a week and missed the grinding she gave him about his betting habits. Up to the Teller's window he sauntered with a shitty little smile on his face and devil in his eyes. She didn't give him a chance to start up. She just chewed him up a little around the edges until the smile was gone from his face.

"I hear you're a big time flatfoot now, driving a fancy car and had the mob chase you around town, shooting at you at all hours of the night. Isn't that mature," she continued. "What type of miracle are you hoping for today, Mr. Grimes?"

"'Here's Hoping' in the sixth," he answered. He got his ticket and moved away, trying to figure out what got her so miffed. "Dames," he muttered to himself.

He walked into the seating area, still trying to figure Stella out, climbed the stairs to his favorite seat and settled in to watch two earlier races before the sixth was due to run.

It was like an old movie that you've seen over and over again. The same people were there, all sitting in their same seats, except of course Geno and his wife. They were all wishing for a better life than they had. People winning, people losing, book makers, knee breakers and of course, Whitie Simms.

Whitie was still that small time hood Lou knew him to be and probably hadn't changed his ways since Lou busted him some time back. Just like always, Lou was sure Whitie was losing only today Whitie was more than just a little agitated as his horse came in fifth and he beat his hands against the fence.

Two gorillas that were sitting with Whitie all this time got up and put their hands on his shoulders. He jumped like he had just touched an electrical wire and backed away from them as if trying to get away.

Lou couldn't hear the conversation, but he was sure it wasn't good for Whitie Simms. He seemed to be pleading with the men, his hands moving wildly in the air and he was trying to make a case for them to let him go.

He must have succeeded because they backed away and Whitie made a mad dash for the turnstiles and freedom.

Lou would later find out that Whitie was into the local mob boss, Terry Donavon for $3,500 and the clock was ticking.

Whitie ran past Lou without looking at him but it seemed that he had seen the Devil himself. He ran out of the track with terror in his eyes, trying to lose himself in the crowds in the street and escape the men who had just threatened his life. He could run home and hide in his room and tell his mom how unfair the world was and everyone was against him. Edith, his mother, would tell him that he was her little boy and everything was going to be all right, which was normally enough for Whitie but these days living at home with his elderly mother for free, having her cook and clean for him and give him money wasn't enough. He wanted the world handed to him and if not, he was going to take it! He always took the money his mother gave him and at the same time complained to her when she hadn't done his wash or made his bed.

She had a job cleaning the washrooms at a local speakeasy down the street and even though she was 65, she never complained. She was up early and home late, but still managed to have his supper on the table whenever he wandered in.

He would always go through her purse each morning and take any money he found there before he left for the day. "She wouldn't miss it," he thought, "she's old, and she thinks I'm a salesman." She was too old to figure it out anyway, he'd tell his friends and besides, working is for chumps.

He needed money and he needed it fast. Donavon wasn't going to wait much longer and his life expectancy was getting shorter and shorter.

He walked down the street with his hands in his pockets and his head in the clouds when he found himself in front of Maude's Diner.

He still had the price of a cup of coffee in his pocket so maybe something would come to mind. Whitie went into the Diner, sat a few booths down from the door, elbows on the table and face in his hands looking into a cup of steamy hot Jo. "How in the hell did I manage to pick yet another nag," he wondered.

Lost in thought, he managed to miss seeing two other guys come into the Diner and sit in the booth next to his. Normally it wasn't a big deal, but these guys were talking loudly at times and Whitie found himself listening to their conversation and getting excited.

They were talking about an old museum on the lower east side off Millar Avenue. They had been told that it was packed with all kinds of loot and practically screaming out "please rob me."

Whitie's ears were tuned into their conversation like sonar in a submarine. He was hearing everything they were talking about.

"It's a quiet little building that's been there for years and doesn't get much foot traffic," the first thug was saying. "The guard there is old and has been working there since the place opened. He has a cot in the back room and I was told by a reliable source, that he sleeps like a rock."

"Should be a piece of cake," the other thug said.

There was more conversation about what was there; coin collections, rare jewelry and probably some cash.

Then they discussed when they were going to pick this low hanging fruit and tomorrow night around 11:00 was decided.

Whitie knew where this museum was. He had seen it many times before and never thought anything about it, now was different. This was a way to get free of Donavon and probably keep some dough for him for once. He'd hit the museum tonight and beat these guys to the prize. He didn't feel bad about taking this job. There is no honor among thieves, just opportunity.

He got up quietly from the booth and tried to leave the Diner with little or no notice but true to Whitie's luck, one of the guys from the next booth glanced up for a second, noticed Whitie as he looked at the pair in the booth and went back to talking to his partner.

Whitie spent the rest of the day and evening getting his tools together that he kept in a bus locker just for times like these, he then cased the museum.

He would go inside, look around at the art and valuables, just like any tourist would do, all the while checking windows and doors for places to get in. He couldn't believe how easy it was going to be.

At the stroke of midnight Whitie entered the museum through the service door in the back, using merely a screwdriver to defeat the lock. It was dark inside so he had to stand still for a minute for his eyes to adjust and control his breathing.

He moved through the rooms with only the light of the street coming through the windows, and managed to locate what he was looking for during his earlier tour. He opened cabinets and display cases with a small lock pick and removed gold and silver jewelry with little effort.

There were a few golden statues, candle holders, and a pen and ink set made of silver. He also noticed in the display case, a piece of rock that had a vein of silver running through it.

He moved quietly to the guard's room and was happy to see that he would not have to hurt the old man over a few things he had no interest in and he moved around the room finishing his business.

Satisfied with his haul, Whitie moved to the back of the museum to leave when he noted an old desk tucked out of the way, near a storage room.

Being the thief he was Whitie could not leave without looking in the old desk. "Who knows what might be there?"

He was not disappointed. The drawers were locked but easily pried open with little to no effort and offered up a couple of coin sets, a small cash box and a display case containing half a dozen rings that looked like they might be worth something.

Whitie was about to leave, but something bothered him about the desk drawer that he couldn't put his finger on. He had emptied the contents of the drawer into his bag, but the drawer's inside did not seem to match the size of the outside and when he had emptied the contents, it still had weight to it and it rattled somewhat. He decided to take another look.

It took only a few seconds for the experienced thief to see that the drawer was hiding a false bottom. He smashed into it with little effort or noise. An old leather bag was all that was there.

The old bag contained nothing but a gun that had seen better days and probably wouldn't fire if he wanted it to. Whitie put it back in the bag and would think about it later. For now he had to get out of the museum.

He got clean away and made it back to his mom's house by about 3:00 AM. He locked himself in his room with his bag of loot and was sitting on the bed when a light knock on his door nearly pulled him out of his skin.

"What?" he yelled a little too aggressively.

"It's me dear," Edith answered softly. "I heard you come in, it's very late. Are you okay? Can I make you something to eat?"

He yelled at her from the other side of the door. "Ma I'm fine, damn it. Go to bed!"

Chapter 14

Whitie woke the next morning with a start and put his hand under the bed to confirm the bag was indeed there and it had not been a dream.

He dressed quickly, locked his room and was out the door before Edith could come out of the kitchen to say good morning and ask him what he wanted for breakfast.

He hopped a trolley and headed to the museum to see if they had discovered the robbery. They had indeed and the Police were all over the building, inside and out, looking for clues.

Whitie stayed back from all the activity and watched as reporters interviewed the Manager and the old guard about what had happened. They could tell them nothing. They hadn't heard or seen anything.

Whitie was satisfied that he'd gotten away scot free and all he had to do now was to lie low for a couple of days and then fence the stolen goods and pay Donavon off.

He moved slowly from the crime scene, trying not to bring attention to himself. He looked across the street and there, standing at the other corner were the two guys he overheard at the Diner the day before and they didn't look happy.

He hoped he'd gotten away without being noticed, but it was hard to say. Time would tell.

He went back home and unlocked his bedroom door. He went right to his bed and looked under it, to see if the bag was still there. It was.

Edith was at work so he went into the kitchen and turned on the radio to see if there was any other news about the robbery. A half hour later the announcement came on with the broadcaster saying that the old Jim Beaton Memorial Museum had indeed been robbed and there were no suspects at this time. An audit was being performed to see what was missing and its value.

Whitie had to control himself and lie low one more day before he could unload his stolen merchandise. He needed a fence.

Chapter 15

Ruby was raging with anger and throwing things around her shop as her two knee breakers stood back and tried to avoid being hit with flying objects.

She was the one who cased the museum for over a week and had arranged for her two animals to break in and take anything that wasn't nailed down. If the old guard got in the way, well that was just too bad for him. It was going to be so simple, even her meatheads could do it. "What went wrong? Someone had double crossed her and they were going to pay."

She just about had a heart attack when her pets, Benny and Alphonse had come to her this morning and said that someone had beaten them to the job and the place was empty.

"Did you talk to anyone about the job?" she asked. "Did you get drunk last night and blab to a dame?"

Both shook their heads and said they had talked to no one.

"Did you go any place?" she asked.

"We just stopped one place yesterday for coffee and talked to each other about the job. There was no one else in the Diner."

Alphonse touched Benny's shoulder. "Remember, I told you, I saw that little shit Simms heading out the door about half an hour before we left."

"Don't know, didn't see him," Benny responded. "Anything's possible."

Ruby had a target. "Find him fast and ask him the right questions. Do you understand?" she said. Her face was bright red and her eyes were black as the night.

Benny and Alphonse looked at each other and didn't ask any other questions.

As they left the shop, she gave them one more warning. "If you don't find him, don't come back."

Chapter 16

Whitie was sitting in the kitchen with the bag beside him when Edith came through the door. She hung her old coat on the nail by the door and put her purse down on the floor next to it. She looked tired, real tired but she hurried into the kitchen, apologizing for being late. It was her boss's fault; he made her stay late to clean up after a party.

"I've been sitting here for hours Whitie complained. There's no supper on the table and I haven't eaten all day."

Edith busied herself frying a couple of eggs and a small piece of ham she had been saving so he wouldn't whine so much and then she could get on with the laundry and make his bed.

The bag at Whitie's side had not gone unnoticed and Edith asked what it was. "It's salesman samples," Whitie said, "nothing important."

Edith could tell when he was lying and this was one of those times.

She missed his father, he had left them a long time ago in a tragic car accident and Whitie was without a man's guidance and had grown up a whining, frail coward but she loved him, he was all she had. Today she was real tired and didn't need any of his shit.

He was up early the next day before Edith could wake up and offer to make breakfast. He checked her purse found that she was hiding the rent money in a small compartment in the back, behind a notebook. He took the money and ran out the door.

If he managed to fence his merchandise today he would replace the money and maybe even give her a little extra.

The fence was located just outside Chinatown, he had been told. It was fronted by a pawn shop called "Ruby's." Whitie had never been there before. He was told that the lady that ran the place was a cold hearted bitch and would probably run the price down if she got a chance. It was something he'd have to deal with.

Edith's rent money was burning holes in his pocket and he didn't want anyone to see him in the open so he took a cab to Ruby's.

He got to the pawn shop about 9:00 AM and entered quickly so as not to be seen.

Ruby came out from the back of the shop and eyed him carefully to see if she could get that "cop feeling vibe" about him. Trust was not one of her strong suits, so she stayed behind the counter, close to the shotgun she had hidden there.

"What can I do for you Mac?" she said, sitting back on her chair. She could see he was nervous. He spent too much time looking out the window rather than getting down to business.

"So what's in the bag slick," she smiled, trying to calm his fears. "My name is Ruby and I run a class joint here and will give you a fair price for what you're unloading," she continued.

"Don't want to pawn anything, I want to sell it," Whitie's voice came out a little too high.

"Well pardon me," she laughed. "What do you have in the bag that I might want to buy?"

Whitie came up to the counter a little too fast and Ruby reached under the counter, putting her hand on the shotgun.

"I've got stuff here you've never seen before lady, and I want top dollar for them or I'm going down the street to your competitor." Whitie puffed out his chest. He didn't know that Ruby ran that pawn shop too but she let it go on anyway.

"My granny died and left me all this stuff in her will and I want to sell it. I need some quick cash; I'm leaving town."

Ruby had heard this story many times before and many others. She wasn't about to swallow any bullshit this little weasel was trying to sell her. She just wanted to see what was in his damn bag.

Whitie began taking objects out of the bag and putting them on the counter in front of Ruby's widening eyes. She came around the counter quickly and went to the front door to lock it and draw the curtains. This was not the time for visitors or unwelcomed guests like the police.

After one look at the street, she turned to her visitor and put on her best painted smile. She returned to the counter and picked up her jeweler's glass that was sitting nearby and put it to her eye. She examined all the beautiful diamonds, gems and rings that were in front of her and immediately knew she had seen them before, in that old Beaton Museum the week before.

It was all she could do to contain herself and not kill him on the spot as she looked upon what was supposed to be hers and not this little chiseler. She knew him now. He was Whitie Simms, a small time nothing thief that was in Maude's that afternoon, heard about the museum and ripped her off.

She could kill him right now and call it a robbery but that would bring unwanted heat on her and she didn't need it at this time.

She focused on the haul in front of her. Her mind was in overdrive trying to come up with a plan to get her property back and teach this bug a lesson he would never forget at the same time.

A light came on in the far reaches of her dark mind and she raised her head and took the glass away. "Fifteen hundred dollars slick, for the whole lot."

Whitie was thunderstruck. "Are you crazy lady, he yelled! There's $10,000 worth of stuff here. That's quality merch in front of you lady, and you know it.

She sat back on her chair and continued with her sales pitch by telling him there was no way this was from his granny's house. "$1,500 and that's my final offer."

"$3,500" Whitie countered.

She shook her head again.

"$2,500" and his voice started to crack.

"$1,500 buster, and that's all you're getting from me."

Whitie was crushed. He exhaled a deep breath, looked down defeated and shook his head, okay, "$1,500" he said, "cash."

She counted out the hundreds in front of him and noted that he was still holding the bag. "Got anything else in there you want to sell?" she asked.

Whitie knew he still had the old gun but right now keeping it was a better idea. He was going to need it for protection.

He put the money in his sack and quickly left the shop, nearly running down the street to put distance between Ruby and himself. He needed to get someplace safe, stop and think about what had just happened and what he was going to do now.

He was in the open again and he knew it. He waited in an alleyway for a trolley to roll by and hopped on it before it could slow down. He went to the back of the car and sat with his back against the wall. This way he could see if anybody got on that might be a problem. He would be aware immediately. For right now he was moving and that was a good thing.

He stayed on the car for the better part of an hour and cleared his head. He had $1,500. That wasn't enough to clear himself with Donavon but it would go a long way in extending his loan payback time or he could leave town right now and not come back but he had no idea where to go; or he could double or triple his money by getting to the track and betting the whole load on a horse he knew was running today that had been juiced with steroids and could win the race going away.

To Whitie it was a no-brainer. He got off the trolley a block away from the track and walked with the crowds up to the gates so he could get inside unnoticed.

He moved quickly to Stella's window and dropped the bag in front of her. She was already annoyed seeing him because he was such a little weasel that didn't know when to stop and go home.

"Everything on 'Lightning Boy' in the fourth race to win Stella." She shook her head at him again and he emptied $1,500 in hundred dollar bills onto the counter and the place went immediately quiet for a second or more.

"Where did you get this money Whitie?" she wanted to know. "It's really dangerous carrying this type of cash around. You know that, don't you?" she said.

"I'm not carrying it around anymore lady, so give me my stubs and make it quick!"

Stella shook her head and gave the little thief his stubs while at the same time calling security to come over and remove the money from her drawer.

Unknown to Whitie at the time, as soon as he laid the cash on the counter, men were moving to telephones and letting people know that Whitie Simms, a small time hood, a nothing, had just laid down $1,500 cash on a horse in the fourth.

The telephone lines went crazy. Word got around quickly and unknown bodies were moving toward the track quickly.

Stella was very unhappy with Whitie and his rash decision to bet all that cash. She wasn't sure what to do until Edith came to mind. Stella wondered if Edith knew Whitie was at the track with all that cash.

The answer was simple, phone her and let her know that her son was making the mistake of his life. She used the phone in her boss's office and contacted Edith right away.

Edith was astounded at what Stella was telling her and called the Lord's name out many times. Then there was silence on the line for the longest time until she finally thanked Stella for her concern and hung up.

Chapter 17

Ruby sat behind her counter and was going red in the face as Whitie walked out of her shop. The little bastard wasn't going to get away with this, she muttered to herself between clenched teeth. "It's not going to be that easy for you, you little turd."

As Whitie was rounding the corner and out of sight, Ruby was on the phone to her two knee breakers, letting them know that she had just bought her own jewels and coins from the robbery that she had set them up to do, by a little street weasel named Whitie Simms. "Does that name sound familiar to you, you two assholes? He played you guys like cheap violins. You chumps better get my money back!" she screamed into the phone and slammed the receiver down.

There was just one other call to make and that was to Donavon but against her better judgment she decided not to.

Donavon liked to keep tight control of his businesses on the south side and his money. Letting anyone make him look bad was bad for business and he dealt with them quickly. He had already heard about Whitie from people at the track, and had dispatched four of his men to find Simms and bring him to his office.

Whitie was to be made an example of and his dead body was to be thrown from a speeding car into the street in front of the racetrack.

Chapter 18

Whitie moved from the ticket wicket down the long ramp and out into the seating area of the racetrack he knew so well over all these years. In his hand he clutched fifteen $100 ticket stubs and in his mind was about to make a fortune. It was hard for him to keep his composure. He didn't want to make a scene, but inside he was going insane.

His whole life had come down to the next few minutes and he was beaming and terrified all at once.

The starting gates burst open with a thunderous crash and the ground shook as the heavy hooves of ten crazed, screaming horses dug into the earth and powered themselves forward.

Whitie could see the crazed excitement in the horses' eyes as they wildly galloped past his location trying to get to the front of the pack all the while being whipped on their asses by tiny little men wearing colorful clothing, holding on for dear life.

Whitie got up and was pressed against the fence, sweating and breathing as hard as the horses. Suddenly his eyes opened wide in disbelief as he watched 'Lightning Boy' break into the open and leave the pack behind.

Two lengths, then four, then six! The horse was a blur. At the half and the three quarter mark 'Lightning Boy' continued to surge ahead. Whitie was slamming his hands into the fence and screaming like a madman. "He's going to win!" he screamed. "He's going to win!"

A heartbeat later, Whitie's world turned upside down as "Lightning Boy" seemed to stutter in his step, stumbled and fell dead on the track before crossing the finish line!

Whitie was destroyed. He was so scared he wet himself where he stood and didn't even notice. What was he going to do? Where could he go?

Then it came to him – run! He had to run and run now! He bolted up the ramp, knocking people down and pushing the rest to the side. Escape! He had to escape was all he could think of.

He became aware that people were watching him, but really not watching him. He knew they were waiting to see what was going to happen next and whether or not he'd even make it to the door. He had to get to the door.

He could feel his world closing in on him. No time left! Then from out of his paranoia he saw a life-line, a friend, or at least someone he trusted, Lou Grimes!

Whitie knew that he and Lou had history, some good some bad. Lou always seemed to be busting him when he was a cop but Whitie knew he was a straight shooter and would help if he could.

Lou wasn't expecting to see anybody he knew today, other than Stella and was taken aback by the sight of Whitie Simms running toward him like a man possessed.

Whitie grabbed him by his arms and began to cry uncontrollably until Lou calmed him and got him talking.

Whitie blurted out that he was in debt to Donavon and his time was running out. The worst thing was that he had lost all the money he had. He was already begging Lou to loan him some money so he could play another horse and this time win.

Lou wasn't about to loan this madman a dime let alone the $25 he had brought with him to play his own hunch. He waved at Stella from across the room as he pushed Whitie away and stood back to give him shit.

Lou looked down at Whitie and asked himself "did he piss himself?"

Whitie was beating his head with his fists, trying to come up with a plan to save his life and was just on this side of having a heart attack. He turned away from Grimes for a second and then turned back, reaching into his pocket.

"What about this Grimes?" he asked, pulling the bag out of his pocket. Whitie opened the bag and showed Lou what was inside. It was a gun. "Should be worth at least $50 to you, shouldn't it?" he pleaded.

Lou found himself looking at an old six gun with a brown walnut handle grip and scrolling down the barrel.

"I'll sell it to you cheap," Whitie's lips were dry but he still had sweat rolling down his face. He was shaking so hard he could barely hold the bag. "Come on Lou," he said.

Lou knew the piece was probably hot but something drew him to the gun that he couldn't explain when he looked at it. "I'll give you $25 you little shit and it's against my better judgment."

Relief flooded over Whitie's face as he handed over the six-shooter, still in the bag and collected his $25. "You saved my life Lou," he said as he quickly blended into the crowd, heading for the betting window to place a wild bet that had no chance of ever winning according to the odds.

That was the last time Lou Grimes saw Whitie Simms alive, running down the ramp to the track fence with stubs in his hand to cheer on his last hope.

Lou just stood there. What was he going to do now he asked himself as he stood in the doorway to the horse track with no money and a gun in a leather sack?

Shaking his head, he finally decided to call it a day and head back to the Biltmore to put his new gun away. From what he had seen of it in the brief second or two, it was going to need some work, but that would have to wait.

Back in his room Lou put the sack in his dresser drawer and walked over to Eddie's to get a beer and a sandwich and read the newspaper. So much for making his fortune today he thought. He still didn't know why he bought the old gun. It was something he couldn't explain but he had to have it.

The afternoon rolled along and Lou got to talking to a lot of people, like you sometimes do at the bar. He also got a call from Abraham around 06:00 PM and was asked to drop by when he could because he had some work for him.

Lou said he'd be around by noon the next day to pick up the file.

Chapter 19

It had been a long day for Whitie it was like an eternity had passed since he left Ruby's and made his way to the track, lost all that money and knowing he was a dead man. Now here he was again, face pressed up against the fence with his ticket stubs in hand, praying for a miracle.

Lou's $25 and what was left of the rent money had brought him to this moment. One more race around the track. Two more minutes of his life and everything he had riding on a horse called "Moment of Madness."

The bell rang, the gates crashed open and in less than two minutes Whitie watched his horse cross the finish line ahead, in front of everybody else! Whitie fell to his knees and cried like a baby for the longest time, before a friend came up to him to see if he was okay.

It was only now sinking in that he had won and things were about to change for the better. His head was in the clouds and he was calmer than he ever thought he could be and he moved towards Stella's window.

Stepping up to her wicket he laid down his winning stubs and forgot to breathe. He still wasn't convinced that he had won until Stella started to count out $25,000 in $100 bills.

"That was the scariest thing you ever did Whitie," she said shaking her head. She put the money in a black bag and slid it across to Whitie's shaking hands. "Get out of here," she said. "Go home and don't come back."

He didn't hear her as he picked up the bag and stepped back. He was already thinking of the things he was going to do, travel maybe.

He wasn't looking where he was going and was startled when he tripped and fell to his knees over a man sitting on the floor. Whitie looked into the face of a man in tatters, a beggar that couldn't look back at him, he was blind. He had a white cane and a piece of paper pinned to his jacket with "Veteran" scrawled on it.

The old man started to apologize for tripping Whitie and was trying to stand up but couldn't. He put his hand on the Veteran's shoulder and said he was truly sorry for not seeing him and asked if he was hurt. "Not really," the beggar replied. "The old legs don't have much feeling in them these days, shouldn't have had them hanging out there like that."

Whitie continued to have his hand on the man's shoulder. "Veteran?" he asked.

"Yes sir," the beggar replied. "Lost my eyes and the feeling in my legs on the beach at Juno in '44' and since then things haven't gone all that well, but I do get by."

Whitie finally realized that he was looking at someone that was worse off than he had ever been. "What's your name Veteran?" Whitie asked.

"Larry," he replied, "Private Larry Crandell USMC, retired, sir."

At that moment Whitie felt something in his chest that he hadn't felt in years – compassion. He reached into the bag and pulled out a $100 bill and put it in the old man's hand. "That's a c-note old timer, have a better day on me. You deserve it."

The old beggar squeezed Whitie's hand and thanked him for being such a good man and God would surely bless him for his act of kindness.

Still thinking about what the old man had just said, Whitie took a few steps back and a few more toward the door and looked up. A surprised look came over his face, then a searing, numbing pain in his side, weakness, calm, darkness, nothing.

Chapter 20

Lou woke the next morning with a spring in his step. He didn't know why, just that his bones weren't aching like they usually did, and his head wasn't as fuzzy as it should have been after trying to drink Eddie's beer stock dry the night before.

Whatever it was, he was okay with it and wasn't going to look a gift horse in the mouth.

He dressed quickly and headed downtown at about 9:30 AM and pulled up in front of Abe's bail bond shop at about 10:00.

Abe was waiting for him and after pleasantries, he received his next file. Sam Talls was arrested for bootlegging homemade gin. Bail was set at $25,000. It was a small job, but to Lou, money was money and this pigeon wasn't going to be too hard to find.

Lou drove back to Maude's and sat in his favorite booth and ordered lunch before opening the file.

"Sam Talls, 45 years old, single, lives with his Aunt, son of an old Arkansas moonshiner that had been selling his father's backyard hooch for many years.

Lou figured it was an innocent enough crime, after all moonshine is just moonshine, but this time the gin made people sick and one even died and that changed everything.

He would want to talk to Sam's Aunt the following day, seeing that she had put up the collateral for his bail.

Grimes had been sitting there for the better part of three hours going over the information and setting up a plan when Shamus came through the door.

Lou could tell something was up because he had that serious cop face on, the one he had when something wasn't right.

Shamus came over, sat down, crossed his large arms over his chest and said "bin looking for you Lou, you're a hard man to find these days."

"You know how it goes, Shamus," Lou came back. "Places to go, people to see; I've been a busy man since you put me to work. What can I do for you buddy? Why were you looking for me," he probed.

Shamus came right to the point. "Whitie Simms is dead."

Lou knew the police tactic that Shamus was trying. He was looking for a reaction but he wasn't going to get one. Lou sat back in the booth, lit his cigar again, taking a little more time than normal so he could process what he had just heard. He pulled hard on his smelly old rope then leaned forward to let the smoke escape and ask the next question.

"What's this have to do with me pal? Am I a suspect?"

"No, Jesus No," Shamus was laughing. "It was just that you saw Whitie yesterday, shortly before he was killed."

"When was that?" Lou wanted to know.

"At the track," Shamus said. "Whitie was killed at the track soon after winning a large sum of money."

"He won?" Lou's voice rose.

"$25,000" Shamus answered "in $100 bills. He played the longest odds in track history and won a fortune. You're not a suspect Lou, but some witnesses say you were talking to Whitie shortly before his death and gave him some money."

"He hit me up for a loan. He was a raving madman so I gave him what I had, $25 and then I left."

Lou didn't tell Shamus about the gun, that would just cause problems that he didn't need right now. "How did he die?" Lou asked.

"He was found slumped over on a bench near the door of the main betting area in a pool of his own blood. He died from a single stab wound to his upper right side, piercing his liver and killing him instantly. They knew what they were doing Lou," Shamus said.

He got up to leave but before going he told Lou to keep him in the loop if he heard anything.

Lou sat there for the next hour trying to take in what he had just heard. He knew Whitie was a piece of work and had rubbed a lot of people the wrong way, but murder?

He drove back to Eddie's to find a full house of wanna-be detectives trying to speculate just how Whitie had died because it wasn't common knowledge. They were also speculating who was responsible and where was all that money?

He wasn't even in the door before people came rushing up to him, getting in his face and asking him if he had heard what had happened. He was getting annoyed quickly, pushing a few away. He needed some beer to calm his nerves, but that wasn't going to happen either because someone was sitting on his stool!

Of all the stools in all the bars in Chicago this lowlife had to be sitting on his stool at this particular time. The guy was 40-something, wore a cheap suit, overcoat and black hat. To Lou, he looked like a salesman that probably just came in to get off his feet so he was about to cut him some slack and just ask him to leave.

That didn't happen. As Lou got close to the man, he didn't even look up from his beer, just sneered at Lou and told him to take a hike. He didn't want any company.

"I don't want to party with you Mac," Lou sneered back. "I just want your ass off my stool."

The salesman turned and was about to say something else, but was met by Lou's hand grabbing his throat and dragging him off the stool to the floor. "I don't want or like any strange asses or strange assholes sitting on my stool Bub. You got that? Or do I have to make it clearer?"

The startled man got up off the floor with his hands outstretched in a defensive pose. He wanted no more of Lou Grimes or his damn stool.

With that Lou settled in on his stool. He knew he was definitely going to look into Whitie's death, but right now he had a skip on the loose and time was money. He had a couple of beers and a shot of whiskey to help him sleep and went off to his room.

He settled in and closed his eyes and awaited sleep to take him but for a split second he thought about the gun in the bag and what he should do with it.

It seemed like only a heartbeat later and he was up early and having coffee after which he jumped in his car to drive across town to Sam Talls' Aunt's house.

It was a small apartment in an old building. Lou knocked on the door for sometime before it opened a crack and a little old woman in her seventies with grey hair tied in a bun, glasses on her nose, bony fingers and wearing an apron peered through.

"What do you want?" she growled at him.

Lou could see right away that she had a nasty temper and for a quick second he wondered what else she had behind the door. "Need to speak to Sam Talls Ma'am," he said in a calm voice.

"He's in jail, now go away," she spat back and tried to slam the door closed.

Lou was too fast for her and had his foot jammed against the door so it wouldn't close. "Now that isn't quite true ma'am, is it?" he smiled back. "You bailed him out two weeks ago and now he's missed his court date. I need to locate him before things get worse for him and you."

"You won't find him, flatfoot," she hissed. "I gave him money to buy a bus ticket to his Dad's place in Arkansas. Now piss off before you lose that foot. You city folk don't understand hill people and you never will." With that she slammed the door hard enough to wake the dead or at least the rest of the neighborhood.

Arkansas was not in Lou's immediate future. It was out of state to begin with and he didn't like buses. They were always full of lowlifes.

He walked back down the hall to the stairway and was trying to convince himself that this one got away and he'd have to tell Abe that he was going to have to throw the old lady out of her apartment and good luck with that. Then a door opened a bit just in front of him and a voice whispered through the crack, "you looking for Sam? What's it worth to you flatfoot?"

"I will give you a sawbuck if you tell me what I want to know." Lou replied.

"Fair enough," the voice replied. "The old lady is blowing smoke up your ass. She gave him money alright, but not for the bus. Sam's hiding down by the docks looking to buy passage on any freighter going anywhere."

Lou slipped the money through the crack. The door closed quietly and Lou made his way back to his car.

The docks were across town and he was behind the curve already. He made it there in half an hour and looked around the vast expanse of ships and containers. This was not going to be easy. He needed a plan.

He sat back and watched the goings on in the dock area for over an hour. There seemed to be some activity down the block at what looked like a bar or a whore house and Lou thought it would be worth a shot.

He walked up to the building and saw a sign in the window "Deckhands needed as soon as possible, apply within."

Lou knew that this was what he was looking for and his instincts kicked in. This was definitely the place. Inside he took a seat at the bar and waited. Late into the night he sat and watched the door for something he knew was coming. He was right again. At about 11:45 the door opened and in walked Sam Talls.

He went right up to the bar like he had been there before and ordered a whiskey while at the same time propositioning one of the girls that worked there. The deal was struck and Sam and the broad headed upstairs but didn't get past the first two steps.

Lou moved quickly from the far side of the bar to the stairs without startling the pair and hit Sam in the back of his head bringing him to the floor with a solid thump.

The girl screamed and continued to run up the stairs and the bartender and a few tough-looking longshoremen moved toward Lou with anger in their eyes.

Lou cuffed his man and turned to the advancing men and said in a low voice "my name is Lou Grimes and this piece of shit is wanted for manslaughter. If you want a piece of this, just keep moving forward and I will accommodate you."

That stopped the men in their tracks. They backed off and sat back down.

Lou stood Sam up, grabbed him by the collar and headed for the door. He looked at the bartender who shook his head and walked to the other end of the bar.

It was late but Eddie's would still be open so after setting Sam down in front of the desk Sergeant and collecting his paperwork, it was time for friendlier faces and something to wash the waterfront out of his mouth.

Tomorrow he would see Abe to pick up his cash but for right now it had been one hell of a long day and he was done.

He walked across the street to the Biltmore like he had done so many times before but this time was a little different. He had a murder to look into. He knew he wasn't a policeman anymore and he could get himself into trouble or even worse, killed. He would need to protect himself if he was going to follow the trail leading to Whitie's killers. He'd need to start carrying a gun and as luck would have it, one was available.

Chapter 21

It was one in the morning and Lou was sitting on his bed looking at his dresser that contained the old gun.

He moved toward it and wondered if the old beast would even fire anymore and it would probably have to be worked on before it was safe.

He took the leather bag out of the drawer and sat on the bed before opening it. The gun looked older than it had before. Lou thought to himself "it must be the lighting in the room."

He reached into the bag and took hold of the old firearm and removed it. It was heavier than he had thought and longer than most guns that were being made today. The barrel had scrolling on it and must have been twelve inches long with a walnut grip. Next to the trigger guard was a maker's stamp, "Bluntline Colt 45, 33909."

"Strange," Lou thought, "so heavy." Then he noticed his hand was getting warmer, almost hot and he was now holding the gun with both hands and the room seemed to spin and melt away in front of him. It was like being on a bad ride at an amusement park and your stomach was about to hurl.

Lou got scared to death and dropped the gun on the bed. The room stopped spinning and he could breathe again. The experience scared the hell out of him as he looked down at the gun and wondered what had just happened.

He had to be sure that he wasn't drugged so he picked up the gun again and again there was heat and the room started to melt and he dropped the gun again. He needed no more out of body experiences tonight so he picked up the gun with a hanky and deposited it back in its bag quickly and then as fast as he could, he got it back in the drawer.

He lay on his bed fully clothed, looking at the ceiling and thinking about what he had just gone through. Once he started to relax and sleep started to come over him, he wondered "where the hell did Whitie Simms get the gun? Bluntline Colt 45 33909, he'd remember that."

PART II

TOMBSTONE

Wednesday, October 26, 1881; 2:45 P.M.

Chapter 22

The wind, always the wind and along with it the dust that rode that wind, like a never ending, out of control buckboard careening down a steep mountain. Tumbleweeds also took this ride in the wind and hit you in the face faster than you could knock it away.

Sometimes there was so much dust in the air it choked out the light of the sun along with the ability to breathe. This was just another day in Tombstone, Arizona.

People moved about in this soup doing what people do in order to get on with their day. These were Plainsmen, Pioneers of the Old West and Prospectors hoping to strike it rich in the silver veins that were discovered here in 1877.

Along with these riches came men that wanted to take the silver away from the honest miners that broke their backs digging it out of the ground.

This type of life was not for the faint of heart and many of them did not survive but those that did were hard and tough and did whatever they had to, whenever they had to.

Law and Order eventually came to Tombstone in the form of three brothers, Wyatt, Virgil and Morgan Earp. They were hell raisers in their earlier days and intimidated people easily.

Each brother, oddly enough was 6'2. Each brother was around 200 pounds and each brother sported the largest, thickest mustache anyone had ever seen. That's where the similarities ended. Each man had their own personalities and used them to their own advantage.

Virgil, the oldest of the three, was quiet and calmer than the other two siblings and would think things through before making a decision but when provoked, he was just as deadly as any of the three. He was a U.S. Marshal in Arizona Territory and also the town Marshal in Tombstone.

Morgan Earp, the youngest brother, looked up to his older siblings like they were sent from above. He was proud of them and would move heaven and earth to please them. He was never far from their side in any situation. He was very personable and always had a smile and a kind word and tipped his hat to the ladies.

On the other side, Morgan was fearless to a fault and never backed down from a fight. Some would say he had that "Earp" look in his eyes when challenged.

Then there was Wyatt, the middle child of Nicholas Porter Earp and Virginia Ann Cooksey.

His goal in life was to be rich, always seeking new adventures and being with his brothers.

He did manage to accomplish two out of the three. He was a fearless frontiersmen, part time teamster, railway man, buffalo hunter and law dog. He had met Bat Masterson in his earlier days. He was one of the few men Wyatt truly admired.

Over time Wyatt became a proficient Faro card player in the saloons he frequented and found it easier to take gold off the card tables than to dig it out of the ground.

Wyatt was a deadly shot with a pistol, fast as lightning, some said. Others said it was the way he stared at you that could freeze a man in his tracks. That black stare he took on, just before his Colt came alive was when you were looking at the devil himself.

Chapter 23

Virgil stood at the bar in the Orient Saloon, sipping a whiskey with his back to them, looking at the reflection of his two brothers in the mirror. He was proud of them. They had come to Tombstone without hesitation when he asked them and had been there for him and had his back throughout all the misery with the Clantons and the McLaureys.

The Clantons and McLaureys were cowboys that worked on a spread just outside of town. They were local bullies and fancied themselves as bad men by rustling cattle and robbing stagecoaches. They wore red sashes around their waists which they said was a badge of courage to show how bad they were and they were proud of it.

Virgil had posted the town off limits to firearms and this angered the gang to new heights. They did not want to give up their guns. They thought they owned the town and no tin star was going to keep them out.

Two cowboys from the gang, Frank and Tom McLaurey had come into town the day before for supplies and had tried to tear the town up but were met with a beating from the Earps.

On October 26 the rest of the Clanton McLaurey gang rode into town and did not leave their guns at the town limit sign.

Ike and Billy were screaming revenge for their brothers' beatings as they rode into town. A shop keeper came to the Orient Saloon where the Earp brothers were playing cards and told them that the Clantons and Mclaureys were down at the end of Fremont Street at the O.K. Corral armed to the teeth and mad as hell.

Wyatt looked up from under his hat brim at the shop keeper. "You tell em we'll be right along and hell's fire is coming with us."

Virgil stepped back from the bar and checked his brand new $2 pocket watch. It was 2:56, he then finished his whiskey. Without looking at his brothers he said "it's time," and he turned toward the saloon doors.

All three brothers stepped out of the Orient onto the wooden plank sidewalk and into the street. The wind, the swirling dust and low visibility made them look like dark specters.

Townsfolk that had watched them from the safety of their shop windows said later that the three brothers looked like undertakers walking down Fremont Street in their black flat brimmed hats with silver bands, black frock coats and vests, clean white shirts and black neckties and their guns tied to their legs.

The streets were empty except for the wind and the dust that played there. The only other sounds that could be heard were the creaky old wooden signs that dotted the main street, blowing in the wind.

It wasn't more than fifty yards down Fremont Street to the O.K. Corral which was just left of a boarding house called "Lil's." The visibility was next to nothing at times as the brothers neared the Corral, they nearly missed seeing their old friend, Doc Holliday as he stepped out of the boarding house door carrying a short barrel shotgun and joining them in the street as they walked by.

"Not your fight Doc," Morgan said over the wind and the sand.

"Oh I wouldn't miss this party for the world Marshall," Holiday called back and pulled the hammers back on both barrels of his weapon.

The four didn't stop moving forward and after about another ten feet Wyatt yelled over the howl of the wind.

"The devil's come calling boys it's time to meet your maker."

Billy Clanton's last words were "this ain't your fight lunger."

Billy was pointing at Doc Holiday, as both barrels of Doc's shotgun exploded and left a huge hole in his chest. He slammed up against the wall and was dead before he hit the ground.

The world exploded around the men and gun smoke, dust and sand was everywhere. There was a hail of bullets and screams of pain were heard over the wind.

Morgan shot Frank McLaurey in the upper chest, causing him to kneel and continue firing into the air sending two rounds through the window of Big Nose Kate's room. It sent her diving to the floor to escape the shattered glass and broken wood. She had been watching the whole thing.

Before Frank died he shot Virgil in the arm and his brother Tom dropped to his knees and shot Doc Holiday in the lower leg. Both Morgan and Wyatt shot Tom McLaurey at the same time, but the last thing he did before dying in the dirt was to shoot the gun from Wyatt's hand.

It was like being struck by a thunderbolt and it sent Wyatt to the ground, rolling in pain and his favorite Colt flying into the air, disappearing in the swirling dust and gun smoke.

When it was all over and the smoke cleared, three men lay dead on the ground, Billy Clanton and Tom and Frank McLaurey.

Ike Clanton and Billy Claiborne, another gang member, were not to be found, they had run away during the fight but Morgan was sure that he had hit Ike in his shoulder.

Wyatt, Virgil and Doc Holiday were all wounded, but would survive to fight another day. For thirty seconds the devil had come to Tombstone.

The wounded lawmen limped away from the gunfight at the O.K. Corral and went back to the Orient Saloon.

Doc Holiday, because of his leg wound, barely made it back to the boarding house and up to his room to Big Nose Kate. She was waiting for him and ran into his arms. All she said was "that was awful Doc."

For the better part of fifteen minutes nothing moved around the Old Corral, just the wind and the sand. The three men lay in the dirt where they had fallen and would stay that way until the town's people got over the shock of what had just occurred. If everyone had not still been hiding in their shops and houses they would have noticed movement from a small stable attached to the Corral area. A strange little old man everyone in town knew as "Bunny" crawled out from behind a grain bin and picked up his beaten down hat from the dust.

His real name was Jimmy Beaton but no one had ever called him that. He was a little man, barely five feet, and had a beard. His sixty plus years on earth had been hard but he was a survivor of anything life had to throw at him.

His clothes were mere rags hanging from his bent body and the holes in his coat let more dust and dirt in than kept out. His teeth had been paining him something awful lately but he didn't have the nickel to go to the undertaker and have him yank them out.

He had nothing to show for his existence but what he was wearing and his best friend for life and business partner, the General. The General was a small little Mexican burro that Bunny had found wandering in the foothills over twenty years before.

Everybody in town new Bunny as a broken down old beggar that panhandled and played the harmonica just outside the saloon and begged for oats for his little burro to eat down at the Corral.

What they didn't know was that Bunny was also a prospector and had been for many years. Every now and then he would slip out of town and travel to his silver claim, two days walk away and continue to scratch in the dirt and tap little pieces of rock away from his claim he had staked out many years before.

He knew there was silver there, he just knew it. Maybe he wasn't getting very much now but he knew in his gut, it was only a matter of time. Then he'd leave Tombstone and never come back, just him and the General.

He had been sleeping behind the grain bin when all the commotion broke out, people screaming, guns firing and men swearing at one another and then silence. If that wasn't enough, something hot hit him on the side of the face stirring him from his hiding place. It felt like a branding iron on his cheek and stayed there until he shook his head and then it fell to the ground.

He forgot about the burning pain on his cheek as he stood up and looked around. Three men lay dead on the ground not twenty feet away. "Where was everybody," he thought. "What had just happened? Who had shot these men and why was his face burning?" He stared at the horror in front of him, trying to take everything in.

He put his hand to his face and it stung like hell. "What had hit him," he thought as he finally looked down.

His eyes opened wide at what was lying at his feet. It was a gun. He bent down and picked up the weapon that had seared his face only minutes ago and looked closer at it.

It was a Colt 45, a special one, like he had heard about some time back. It had a long barrel, longer than most and a walnut handle. He continued to look at the gun and the dead men only a few feet away and a thought came to him that scared him to death.

"This looks like I killed these men," he thought. "Who in this town is going to believe the word of the town panhandler? This was Tombstone for Christ's sake. They hang people for shit like that here and quickly. There's no way the Marshal was going to see it any other way," he thought.

Panic set in and Bunny began to sweat. "I have to get out of here now!" was all he could think of.

Turning to the General, he placed the gun in one of the side packs, tightened everything down and was gone in seconds.

It was a good time to visit his claim, he thought, while all this mess was going on. That's just what he did, just him and the General.

Life was always simpler for Bunny and the General when they were on their claim. There was nothing to do if you didn't want to.

His claim was located some ways away from Tombstone in a dry gulch that had become overgrown with bush and was away from prying eyes.

Bunny's camp was set up comfortable enough for him. There was a lean-to for weather, water in the form of a small stream and enough jerky and grain to last many months.

Bunny had always gotten silver in small amounts over the years so the camp was easy to maintain. The town's people didn't need to know about this though. To them he was just an old irritation that was always hanging around looking for handouts and playing his harmonica. He liked it that way.

Life goes on, like it does and Bunny and the General had been back to their claim for the better part of the spring. He had sat by his small fire at night many times and looked at the gun that had come into his life that fateful afternoon. It was definitely a Colt and still had two shells in the chamber. He wasn't sure what he was going to do with it right now, but a little protection out at the claim was always welcome.

Bunny always slept well under the stars and this night was no different. He woke early like he always did and boiled some coffee, chewed a piece of jerky and headed down into his mine.

The silver streak that he had been following for the last couple of seasons stilled continued further into the mine, about fifty yards from the entrance so light was there whenever he was working.

He could always get enough silver from his mine to get by. What more could he ask for. He tried to forget what had happened that day in Tombstone and concentrated on the task at hand but it always kept creeping back into his thoughts.

One morning, he worked for a few hours chasing his streak down the wall, not really thinking of anything. It was always the same, force the chisel into a seam or crack and hit it with a hammer; chisel seam hammer, chisel seam hammer.

Every now and then a piece of rock would break off and Bunny would put it into his sack to examine later and bring to the Assayer to sell. Around noon he was thinking about coffee and a break but he had been watching his seam get wider and the silver streak get wider. The chisel fit nicely into the opening and with one more mighty blow, a large piece of rock broke away falling to the ground, damn near breaking his foot, it was so heavy.

He managed to avoid the accident by stepping aside quickly but fell to the ground doing so. He chuckled to himself as he sat up and brushed the dust off, coughing, waiting for the air to clear.

"I'm too old to keep doing this shit," he thought and coughed again.

It was a huge piece of rock that broke away from the wall and lay at Bunny's feet. His vision cleared, and the secret of Bunny's mine finely revealed itself by nearly blinding him as the sunlight gleamed off a pay streak in the rock and on the wall at least a foot wide. It was silver!

He had been a prospector all his life and had spent many of those years crawling in and out of dusty old mine shafts looking for what he had just found! A tired relief came over him and he smiled to himself knowing that it had not all been for nothing.

His feeling of gladness was immediately overtaken by fear and suspicion as he finally realized that what he had, other men would want if they knew he had it.

He broke the large slab up into many smaller pieces that could be easily carried to the Assayer's office in Tombstone where he would sell them and leave town quickly.

It was easy to move around unnoticed. He was Bunny, the harmless beggar and to everyone an all round pain in the ass.

He spent the next three days hiding the opening to his mine with rocks and bush and making it look like no one had ever been there.

Then he loaded the General and began the long walk back to Tombstone.

Chapter 24

It took him the better part of three days to get back to Tombstone. He was tired and his damn cough wasn't going away, which hampered his travel.

He ambled back into town early on the third day and like normal, he went to the Assayer's office and waited for it to open. Anybody that knew Bunny had seen this scenario before, many times.

Ben Thompson, the town Assayer wasn't surprised to see Bunny sitting on his doorstep. He had been there many times over the years.

Ben smiled at Bunny as he opened the door and asked him at the same time how the General was doing these days.

Bunny chuckled and told his friend that the General was getting old and cranky and wasn't pulling his weight. He needed to retire.

"So do you, you old bugger," Ben came back. "You're too old for this kind of shit."

Bunny got to his feet, coughed a few more times and threw his saddle bags over his shoulder. Ben put on his official Assayer's hat and sat down behind the desk.

Bunny came up to the desk and sat quietly looking at the small scale that Ben had put in front of them. "How did you do this time Bunny?" which was his standard question.

"Not too bad Ben," he chuckled. "But you're going to need the big scale today."

With that he poured out the contents of his bag minus one of the four pieces. He was going to keep that one.

Ben's eyes opened wide and he removed his fancy hat. His mouth hung open and he moved forward to loom directly over the three large pieces of rock that were covered heavily in silver. "My god Bunny, where did you get all of this?" was all he could say.

"My claim finally came through Ben. I think I can retire now," he answered. "I need to sell these pieces then I need to know what the claim can assay out by using these three pieces as a marker.

Ben needed a glass of water before he began and locked the front door before he sat down.

It took him a few minutes to weigh the silver ore, minus the rock, but when he was done he sat back and looked at Bunny in a new light.

"You're a rich man Bunny. I can give you $5,000 right now and an Assayer's report stating that your mine is worth over $100,000 and maybe more based on these samples."

Bunny stood up. "You oughta know Ben, my real name is Jim Beaton and the Assayer's report should be made out to that. I don't want to carry that kind of money on me. Makes me a target, if you know what I mean. Can you give me $500 cash and a note to the bank to credit me when I need more?"

That's the smartest thing that Ben had ever heard coming out of this man's mouth for as long as he had known him.

Bunny put the money in his saddle bag and was about to leave when he turned to his old friend and said "Ben, this can't get out too soon. It'll start a panic and I don't need that right now."

Ben agreed and promised to keep Bunny's secret as long as possible and with that Bunny ambled out the door.

He was no fool, being a miner this long had shown him what could happen if you spend too long in the ground breathing all that dust and whatever else was in that dust.

Many people he knew that had worked within the mines over the years were no longer here because they coughed their way into early graves. Bunny knew in his gut what was ailing him but he had to hear it for himself, from a professional sawbones and soon.

He heard that there was someone in Tucson who knew a lot about breathing ailments and was supposed to be real good, so he decided to get to Tucson as quickly as possible.

He gave the General to a friend who worked in the stables, then slowly walked over to the stagecoach office of the Wells Fargo Company and bought a ticket, one way to Tucson, leaving in the morning.

Bunny would probably not be returning and since he was leaving soon, tonight he was going to treat himself to some store bought clothes, a nice room in the Palace Hotel overlooking the street, a barber shave and a bath, maybe two. He would have a steak dinner in the Diner and finally a brandy and cigar on his balcony, watching the sun go down.

He never felt so good or slept so well on his last night in Tombstone.

Chapter 25

Bunny was up at dawn and went to the Hotel dining room, enjoyed breakfast and read the paper.

It didn't take long for word to get around that Bunny had come into some money and the locals wanted to know where he got it.

The stagecoach would leave at 9:00 AM sharp. That meant Bunny had at least an hour before leaving. He had already been interrupted twice by people he didn't know asking him where he had been and where he was going.

When it was finally time to go Bunny walked to the Stagecoach office and was aware that many people on the street were watching him. Word travels fast in a small town.

He opened the office door and was about to enter when he ran right into the town Marshall, Virgil Earp who was coming out of the office and was looking for him.

"Lookin for you Bunny," he said. "Word around town is that you struck it rich on your claim and you're leaving town. Is that true?"

"It's all true Marshall," Bunny said. "It's time for me to get along. I have to talk to a sawbones in Tucson, been feeling poorly lately."

Virgil looked down from his 6'2 height to the small man that stood in front of him. "It's been good to know you Bunny. I hope you get well soon. It's been a pleasure knowing you." Virgil shook his hand and walked away.

Bunny walked into the holding area of the Wells Fargo Stagecoach Company to a small room that had a few people sitting in it. Passengers he assumed that were also heading for Tucson.

There was a lady with a feather hat, a salesman for sure with his little suitcase and another man that looked like a gunfighter. Bunny would be watching him.

There was a loud noise from outside the little room and a dust cloud rolled in. The stagecoach had just arrived.

"Yo Mary, Yo Jim! All of you settle down or I'll sell ya to the glue factory in Tucson!" the driver yelled from the top of the stage. "If you're comin, come on then. I've got a schedule to keep and it doesn't include looking after you wet noses."

Bunny looked out the window just as the dust was beginning to clear to the driver's box of the massive stagecoach. It was a woman! At least he thought it was a woman.

Josephine Buttle was her name, born 35 years ago to a Navaho Squaw that liked whiskey and men too much and a mountain man named "Wild Cat Billy." She was raised by three older brothers that were tough as rawhide and teased her unmercifully every day. It turned her hard, real hard and she didn't trust anybody.

Most people around knew her as "the Badger." If you called her by Josephine or ma'am it would get you a punch in the face or at least a bottle broken over your head. She was mean as a snake and badger combined and just as deadly with that Arkansas toothpick she carried in her belt or the Smith and Wesson Revolver she wore high on her shoulder.

When she was drinking she was a mean drunk, not to be crossed at anytime and she didn't need any company. When she started mumbling how much she hated men, it was time to stay away.

Bunny walked onto the platform and glanced one more time at the driver before entering the stagecoach.

He noted she wore a buffalo robe coat with a large collar and a mule skinner hat pulled down low over her ears and tied under her chin. A red checkered shirt and matching bandana could be seen under the open coat.

Her Smith and Wesson gun was always visible and a double barreled shotgun hung over the back of her seat. The heavy leather gloves she wore completed her outfit and were holding six thick leather reigns in one hand that were connected to six very large black horses that were eager to get moving. She held a long black bullwhip in the other.

"Get in if you're coming!" she yelled. "This is your last warning."

The passengers were barely sitting down when the Badger yelled loudly at the team to move out and cracked the whip over the terrified horses' heads.

The stagecoach came to life by rising up its front end and swaying dangerously left to right until settling down into a gentle rolling that the road produced.

The trip would take thirty hours so dinner and an overnight stop was laid on at a weigh station some fifteen hours down the road called "Marley's." They would rest the night and a fresh team of horses would be swapped out for the rest of the journey to Tucson.

Chapter 26

The first part of the trip was uneventful, a get-to-know-you as it were. The lone female passenger, a Miss Beth James, was the owner of a boarding house on the outskirts of Tombstone and was heading to Tucson to look at the purchase of another house to expand her business.

The man Bunny thought was a salesman was exactly that. Jim Towns was on his route selling ladies' corsets.

The gunman was Frank Sills. He loved to play poker and hired out his gun for money to finance his love for the game. He was on his way to Tucson to play in a high-stakes' poker game and according to him, he was going to win.

Bunny kept to himself as much as possible. He was coughing more though, the dust was unbearable.

Marley's was a welcome relief after 15 hours of bouncing around in a wooden box. It was a horse ranch located in the foothills of Arizona that sported six bedrooms, a bunkhouse and the best cook this side of the mountains.

Clare Marley was a fabulous cook and innkeeper. She had the guests washed up, fed and resting by the fireplace in no time. Everyone was beat so lights out came early.

Badger took her meals and slept in the stable wanting to be near her animals. She said they were better company and didn't say much, which is what she preferred. Everyone agreed with her choice because the consensus was that she needed a bath; she really needed a bath.

They were all up before the dawn and in the coach ready to go. Clare had given them a country breakfast of potatoes, eggs, steak and biscuits and all the coffee they could drink; along with extra in baskets to eat along the way. Marley's would be hard to forget.

From her perch on top of the stagecoach, Badger yelled out as loud as she could "let's get movin! We're burning daylight!"

With that she slammed the reigns down hard on the backs of her fresh team and let fly her black bullwhip into the gray sky creating an awful crack just above the heads of the lead horses. They were gone in seconds, down the road heading for Tucson.

The Taggit brothers, Tom and Edgar, locals from the Tombstone area had ridden all night to get ahead of Badger's stagecoach. They had been in town the day before and had heard about the old beggar striking it rich and how he was on his way to Tucson before anyone could ask him where his claim was.

It wasn't fair, the old bum having all that silver and money when there wasn't five cents between the both of them. They hatched a plan together quickly to hold up the stage in the hills, take what was rightfully theirs and kill the little bastard if that's what it took.

They were lying in hiding in the rocks of a sharp bend that would make the stagecoach slow down to a crawl to negotiate the turn.

Badger had been down this road a few times and was aware of the sharp turn, but not that the bandits were waiting there to rob the stage. She pulled back on the reigns to slow the team before she heard the crack of a rifle shot and was shocked to feel a stabbing pain in her left shoulder that nearly sent her over the back of the seat and onto the ground.

Gunfire opened up from both sides of the stagecoach, catching it in the crossfire of deadly lead.

The stagecoach came to a stop right were the bandits wanted it and they opened fire on Badger and the people inside the coach.

Badger managed to get down into the boot of the coach, just under the seat and trained her shotgun on the rocks to the left. Both barrels exploded at the same time, spraying the rock face with hundreds of pieces of hot lead and for a second she thought she heard a slight whimper.

Frank Sills opened up, firing both of his Colts into the rock and bush where he thought he had seen a muzzle flash. Even Miss James aimed her Derringer into the rock cover and fired like she knew what she was doing.

Taylor had no gun so he lay down on the floor of the coach hoping to survive the attack.

Bunny pulled the long-barreled Colt from his bag and fired the two rounds that were left in the cylinder after the gunfight at the O.K. Corral.

Sills saw that Bunny didn't have any bullets left and quickly handed his new friend a handful of shells. "It works better when you put these in it," he said with a smile.

The gunfire stopped as quickly as it started and the quiet set in. A few minutes later a voice from the rocks called out "give us the old man and no one else has to get hurt. Have him step out and you can ride away safely."

Everyone in the coach looked at Bunny with surprise. "You must have really pissed these guys off, Mister," Sills said. "They want your ass bad."

Badger poked her head up from the safety of the box and yelled "I don't believe I'll be handing over any of my passengers to any of you skunks today. They paid full fare and I intend to deliver them to Tucson."

"Hand over the little bastard and save yourself more pain, you ugly little witch," Edgar yelled from cover.

With that, the brothers rushed the stagecoach from both sides in hopes of surprising the occupants. That would be the last stupid thing the would-be robbers would do.

Tom left his cover first, hoping to surprise the Badger with such a bold move and shoot her dead before she realized he was there. A fatal mistake on his part cost him his life. Unknown to him, the Badger was watching him break cover from a crack in the side of the boards and cut him in half with both barrels of her favorite weapon, causing his broken body to flip backwards into the bush.

Edgar was a little luckier in his attempt to attack the coach. He managed to climb onto the stage doorstep and look into the coach, only to find himself staring into the barrel of a deadly 45 caliber Colt that unbeknownst to anyone was once the property of Wyatt Earp.

He screamed at it and tried to make a grab for the barrel but a hole appeared in the centre of his hand and another between his eyes. He was dead before he hit the ground.

They dragged Edgar's body into the bush and left him there with his brother. In a day or two a pack of coyotes would probably find them and their existence would fade away into a memory spoken over a card game for many years.

Miss James convinced Badger to come down from her perch on the stage and doctored her wound all the while listening to her complain that her schedule was all screwed up and they had to get moving.

She climbed back up into her seat and she looked down at Bunny and said "are you expecting any other company up ahead, old man? Or can we get on with this trip?"

"I hope not," he said and climbed back into the coach.

Things were settling back down and the adrenalin was starting to wash away. Everyone was quiet in their own thoughts. "What if they had not been that lucky? What if today had been their last day? Would they be missed? Would anyone care?"

Bunny sat there quietly but his thoughts were a million miles away and more than twenty five years earlier. He was full of piss and vinegar back then and had dreams of making it big in the gold and silver mines of Arizona. He was a handsome young buck some said and could catch the eye of many a young filly, if he had a mind to.

He hadn't planned it, it had just happened. He had just arrived in Tombstone, had been riding for two days to get there and was hungry. He rode down the middle of town and stopped at a saloon that had a sign outside that read "Rooms and Dining available."

He walked into the dining room and there she was, serving breakfast to loud obnoxious cowboys that were more interested in having her sit on their laps than eating food.

She was quick and had a way of slipping away from them with a laugh and a smile, so as not to offend them and get on with her job.

Bunny remembered sitting down by the window and watching her work the room. She knew exactly how to play these boys to get the most money out of them with little or no effort, "a pro," Bunny thought, "and at such a young age."

She really wasn't looking at him as she glided over to his table and was about to go into her act. "What can I get for you cowboy?" she began. "The special for today is…" That's where she stopped. His smile caught her by surprise and for a moment she lost her train of thought and smiled back.

"Breakfast, Lunch, Supper, it doesn't matter," Bunny said. "I'll be here for all of them as long as you're here to serve them to me. The name's Beaton, Jimmy Beaton. You can call me Jimmy if that suits you."

"Well Jimmy Beaton, my name is Millie Strong and you can call me Miss Strong."

"I like you're fire Miss Strong," he laughed. "But your table service needs a lot of work."

She stepped back a little shocked, but before she could blast him for being so insulting, he smiled again and said "you didn't even ask me if I wanted coffee first."

This completely caught her off guard and she laughed out loud as she left the room to put in his order.

That moment began an intense two month long romance of long rides in the evening, quiet dinners, walks in the moonlight and love. Jimmy had called it a "wind devil romance." That's when a prairie whirlwind picks up two small pieces of paper off the ground and spins them wildly around and around and up and down, closer and closer until the wind stops or changes directions and the papers fall to the ground, sometimes miles away from each other.

That was the way it was for Jimmy and Millie when the wind stopped. He wanted to continue to prospect and she wanted to leave Tombstone so bad she could taste it. Neither one of them would change their minds.

Bunny remembered the night she told him she was leaving the next day on Charlie Rimms' Wagon Train full of gold hunters, supplies and prostitutes heading for Deadwood, South Dakota. It was there that she would stake her claim and run her own business.

He remembered watching her Wagon Train roll out into the desert and over time disappeared into the distance. To this day he wondered if he had made the right decision to not follow her.

He would have had a life with her, happy most likely, but here he sat in this miserable coach clutching an old letter he had received from her years ago telling him that she had had a child, his child soon after she got to Deadwood. Her name was Victoria and she was the spitting image of him.

He remembered the day he got the letter, so many years ago. You could have knocked him over with a feather, instead here he was making this useless stagecoach journey to a town he didn't know to a doctor he didn't know that was going to tell him what he already knew.

Chapter 27

Tucson was finally on the horizon. Everyone was tired and dirty and ready to be done with the Wells Fargo Stage Line.

Badger was beating the team like she had lost her mind, using the reigns to slap the horses on their backs and her bullwhip cracked loudly in the evening air. She was late and really pissed off about it.

She brought the stage into town at breakneck speed and came to a halt in front of the Fargo office and she jumped down from the seat like she wasn't injured at all. "We're here!" she growled "get out of my coach!

With that she slammed through the front door and was in the process of tearing the man behind the counter a new asshole for what had happened to throw her off schedule.

The tired passengers started coming through the door and Badger was on her way out. "Get out of my way you wet-nosed dudes! I need a drink." With that comment she was gone.

Bunny had had enough adventure to last him a lifetime. Right now he needed a meal, a bath and a drink and couldn't decide which one was coming first. A drink won the argument and Bunny stepped into the nearest saloon. He went up to the bar and ordered a double.

A quick glance around showed him that the Badger had not chosen the same saloon to drink in which calmed him even more, so he ordered another.

A hot meal of homemade beef stew and steaming biscuits and finally a bath was all he needed to end the day perfectly. He slept like a baby. The sun was just coming up but Bunny was already in the dining room with a hot cup of coffee in front of him. He was just finishing up a plate of steak and eggs which he ate like it was his last meal.

It was only a short walk down the sidewalk to the doctor's office but to Bunny it was the longest walk he had ever taken.

He had prepared himself for this long ago when the cough first came on but as he walked through the door clutching the old letter and thinking of Millie, he was scared as hell.

He came into the waiting room and noticed how quiet it was. It was a little on the dark side and smelled like cleaning fluid or something he didn't recognize.

There were all kinds of certificates on the wall from all kinds of places and schools Bunny had never heard of. He figured he must be in the right place.

As soon as he sat down in one of the fancy chairs that was provided and was sinking into, a tall well-built man in his early 50's came through a heavy curtain.

"Can I help you?" he said with a smile.

Bunny rose from his chair and walked over to the man extending his hand. "Hello there doc," he replied. "My name is Jim Beaton. I sent you a telegram some time back and said I'd be dropping by."

"Mr. Beaton, hello," the doctor replied. "Yes, I remember you now."

It didn't take the doctor long to confirm what Bunny had known for quite some time. He was dying. The dust and dirt that he had been breathing all these years while digging in the mines had taken its toll and had been full of arsenic and other poisons that he should never have been breathing.

"Advanced lung cancer," was about to claim what was left of his life and it was going to happen soon.

That day Jim Beaton did something he hadn't done in years. He went to church. No one was there; he didn't need the company. He just sat in the back pew and tried to make sense of it all.

He had worked hard all his life, sacrificed everything to finally get what he wanted most in the world only to have it taken away before he could enjoy it or do something good with it.

He had decided to stay in Tucson, "good a place as any, when you're going to die."

He wondered if the priest here would say a few words over his grave. He would have to ask. He wondered if anyone would morn, seeing as he was alone. That's when a warm feeling came over him and a smile crossed his face. "Millie Strong," he thought. "If only things had been different. It was a lifetime ago and now time was running out."

Jim stood up and looked to the front of the church. "I'm not in the ground yet," he said out loud and walked out into the street to feel the warm morning sunshine. Coffee, he needed coffee.

He had things to do and he had to get started now. He knew that Millie had gone to Deadwood over 25 years ago. That's where she wanted to be and Jim had to bet on the fact that she was still there.

He went down to the telegraph office and sent off a message to Millie Strong, Deadwood City in care of the local Post Office.

It was a simple message with a lot of meaning.

"Millie, it's Jim Beaton. I'm in Tucson. I'm sorry for not following you that day. Biggest mistake I ever made. Second mistake was never meeting our daughter Victoria. My time is short and I need to see you one last time. Please come as soon as you can, Jim."

The telegrapher sent it off right away and promised Jim that when he got a reply he'd send it right over to the boarding house he was going to be staying at.

Bunny wasn't sure that she would come or even get the message, but he had to try.

The next couple of days were busy for Jim Beaton. He had a plan and it kept him focused. The doctor had given him something to calm his cough and ease the ever-mounting chest pain but he had to rest too. Something inside him said that he didn't have time to rest. That would come later.

He went to the Assayer's office and cashed in his last piece of ore which weighed out to be worth $6500. He let the Assayer see the report from Tombstone showing the net worth of his mine.

The man was very interested when Jim said the mine was for sale and promised to get the word out about the find.

Next, Jim took his money over to the bank and made a deposit asking that any money from Tombstone be transferred here. He also had a meeting with the Bank Manager and showed him the mine report hoping that he might know of a buyer.

The banker was really excited and said that he'd get the word out too and get back to Jim shortly. Before leaving the bank his new found friend welcomed him to Tucson.

Word got around quickly that there was a man in town who had struck it rich and suddenly Jim had all kinds of new friends. Mostly they were just people that wanted a handout, giving him their own hard-luck stories. Others who were grifters wanted to know where his mine was so they could "help" him.

A month had gone by with no word from Millie. He ached inside but on the other hand Jim's mine was sold to a group of investors that had gotten together with the bank and now Jim was a very wealthy man.

With all the sudden wealth came responsibility. He needed to get his affairs in order. Each day he visited the doc and each day he was given the long face and was told to rest and to take it easy.

He now had a group of lawyers that took care of his everyday business and he had his Last Will and Testament made up leaving a small sum of money to the church that was going to look after his gravesite after he was gone.

Finally, the bulk of his estate he was leaving to his one true love, Millie Strong from Deadwood, South Dakota or their daughter Victoria.

As fate would have it and unbeknownst to Jim, Millie, his one true love had passed peacefully away in her bed some months prior, of pneumonia so his telegram stayed in her letter box unopened.

Chapter 28

To Millie's surprise shortly after she arrived in Deadwood she found out she was with child. This did not slow Millie down in the least. She amassed a small fortune not long after getting to Deadwood by partnering up with an older lady that knew this type of business.

They purchased an old whore house and fixed it up to become one of the premiere houses on Prostitute Row. Victoria was born in this house but was always shielded from what went on there.

Millie mailed a letter to her long-lost love telling him that he was the father to a beautiful baby girl and not to worry. She was being well looked after.

Millie never married and when Victoria turned 12 years old she decided to send her beloved daughter away to a boarding school in Chicago to get a better education than what she would get in Deadwood.

They stood on the platform holding hands with Millie finally confiding to her daughter that her father was living in Tombstone. His name was Jimmy Beaton and he was a miner there. If anything was to happen to her, she was to contact him. Then she put Victoria on the train and watched as the train pulled away.

By Millie's recollection, that was 15 long years ago last month and she lay in her sick bed having her friend write the letter for her to her daughter asking her to come home quickly. She knew her time was short and wondered why she hadn't asked her sooner. That had been three weeks ago and as the letter traveled east by train Millie quietly passed.

Chapter 29

Victoria was tall for a woman, 5'10, slender and ramrod straight. She had long curly brown hair that was parted in the centre, pulled back in a bun with curls covering her ears. She wore a tight bodice with a high neck and a button down front of white lace that was also on the collar and cuffs of her wide sleeves on a long bell shaped dress. She wore a large bonnet with a lace veil and gloves.

By the time Victoria received the letter from her mother six weeks had passed. She had no idea her mother had already died. All she knew was that she had to get home as quickly as possible. She quit her employment as a governess for a wealthy Chicago family and bought a one-way ticket to Deadwood, South Dakota.

Thanks to her mother, she had completed her education at one of the better colleges in Chicago that accepted women. She had graduated high in her class but was always being admonished because she challenged what the professors were teaching and asked questions they could not answer.

She was definitely her mother's daughter and loved and missed her deeply. The trip back to Deadwood would take a very long time even though train travel was much better than before.

Her friends in Chicago didn't want her traveling alone, seeing that she was a single woman but this didn't deter Victoria in the least. She was going home!

She packed her belongings that included a pair of leather bound journals she had been writing in since she had left home and would no doubt have entries to make during her trip.

The trip took what felt like forever but after weeks of travel the train finally came into Deadwood Station.

She hadn't been home in fifteen years but she knew where she was and how to get to her home.

The wagon pulled up to a huge building on Prostitution Row with three floors and a massive brightly colored sign attached to it that read "The Purple Orchid."

She knew the place well, she had spent her childhood here and it was full of wonderful memories. She walked through the front door and was confronted by a large painting she had seen many times before of her mother and her partner Belle, Kansas City Belle to be precise. They were sitting in large high back chairs looking very formal.

She moved past the painting and turned left into the parlor that had been decorated like a palace with three or four girls sitting around in silk lingerie waiting for customers.

Belle was sitting behind a large oak desk with her head bent down looking at a stack of papers.

She was still attractive to say the least, with her long black hair, high cheek bones and snow white perfect skin. She looked up as Victoria entered the room and started to smile as she recognized the little girl that she had regarded as her own daughter.

Victoria saw her and quickly moved forward to embrace her. "I've missed you so much Belle. How is mother doing? Is she any better?"

Belle stepped back from her embrace and Victoria looked into a face that was grief stricken. She hugged Victoria again and spoke to her softly. "She was really sick Victoria, and really tired. I sat and talked to her everyday and she had me write the letter to you. She tried to hold on till you got here but she was too weak and passed away in her sleep some time back. I'm so sorry child, she loved you very much."

Victoria was stunned by the news and cried for some time in Belle's arms. They sat and talked for hours and then Belle took Victoria to Millie's gravesite.

It was beautifully laid out with white rocks and flowers growing everywhere and there was a beautiful headstone with her mother's name carved deeply into it.

A bench had been positioned near the gravesite, and they sat there for what seemed like forever, talking about Millie and what she had accomplished and how much she loved her Victoria.

From there Victoria was shown to her mother's room to rest.

The next day Victoria came to Belle's office and was given Millie's Last Will and Testament. She had left all of her property and possessions to her daughter along with a sizeable inheritance of more than $50,000.

Prior to Millie passing away Belle had bought her share of the house and that money was also sitting in the bank waiting for Victoria.

It was very overwhelming for her and she told Belle that she would go back to her mother's room to lie down.

Before she could leave the office Belle reached behind her desk and produced a leather sack that contained what Belle thought might be letters and dealings Millie was involved with just before her passing.

She gave Victoria the bag and told her to take her time before making any decisions as to what she wanted to do.

For the next five days, Victoria spent time at the gravesite with Belle, talking about her life in Chicago. She was sure that she'd be returning there but didn't know when.

Victoria was coming to terms with the fact that Millie was gone and there was little holding her in Deadwood so she started making plans to return to Chicago.

She had cleared up Millie's affairs at the bank and wire transferred the moneys there by Western Union to her bank in Chicago.

She was in the middle of packing her mother's personal things, jewelry and such when she remembered the package Belle had given her that contained her mail. She took the package and went down to the gravesite. She wanted to feel closer to her mother and it seemed that reading the letters to her would do just that.

It was junk mostly, letters confirming things that were coming in and others offering her things to buy but it was always the same, people asking for money.

Then Victoria came upon a telegram that was simply addressed to "Millie Strong, Deadwood South Dakota.

She opened it, read it and her heart ached with sadness and she began to cry.

"Millie," it read "it's Jim Beaton. I'm sorry for not following you that day. Biggest mistake I ever made. Second mistake was never meeting our daughter Victoria. I'm in Tucson. My time is short and I need to see you one last time. Please come as soon as you can, Jim."

Victoria was devastated. The sadness she was feeling was almost unbearable, but now she had to go to Tucson and see her father for the first time in her life and tell him about the loss of her mother and his only one true love.

She showed Belle the telegram and told her she was leaving right away for Tucson to be with her father.

Since there was no train station in Tucson yet, she'd have to travel by stagecoach for three days to get there. She said goodbye to Belle and thanked her for everything she had done for her mother and for herself and boarded the coach with one purpose in mind, to be with her father.

Chapter 30

The stagecoach ride was a dirty, dusty ride from hell but the driver finally yelled from his seat that Tucson was dead ahead.

The horses galloped into town and came to a wheel screeching stop in front of the Wells Fargo Stagecoach Office.

After the dust settled, Victoria was helped down by one of her fellow passengers and her luggage set down on the walkway. The town Sheriff was standing nearby, watching the new arrivals exit the coach when Victoria approached him and asked "do you stand there every time the stage comes into town?"

The Sheriff nodded his head and tipped his hat to the very pretty young woman. "Yes ma'am," he replied, "it's part of my job to make sure no undesirables decide to make Tucson their new home."

Victoria smiled back at him. "Are you traveling alone ma'am?" he asked. "That's a dangerous thing to do in these parts."

Victoria told him she could take care of herself and produced a silver Derringer from her bag. "All the same ma'am," he said "it's not a good idea to travel alone. Just doin my job and letting you know," then he started to move away.

Victoria stopped him by putting her hand on his arm, "thank you for your concern Sheriff but can I ask you a question? Do you know if there is a Jim Beaton in town? I am his daughter and have come a long way to see him."

The Sheriff took out his pocket watch from his vest pocket and snapped it open. He looked at it for a minute or two and then replied without looking at her. "Got to get on with my rounds ma'am," he said and stepped away but then stopped without looking at her. "You might want to talk to Mrs. Hemsley over at the boarding house. She will know where he is."

Victoria's heart began to beat wildly. She was finally going to meet her father. She had so much to tell him including the fact that Millie, his one true love, had passed away.

She hired a buggy that was standing in front of the Wells Fargo Office to take her to Mrs. Hemsley's Boarding House and was in front of a modest two storey white house in a matter of minutes.

After being helped down from the buggy, she walked up to the porch half expecting to see her father sitting in a rocking chair drinking a hot cup of coffee. What she got instead was an elderly looking woman, about five feet, a little on the heavy side, grey curly hair that was pulled back in a bun. She wore an apron and a big friendly smile. Her hands and arms were covered in flour so she must have been in the middle of baking.

Victoria approached and the lady of the house wiped the flour off her hands onto her apron and opened her arms in a welcoming gesture. "Welcome to my home young miss, my name is Emily Hemsley. You can call me Emmy."

Victoria smiled back at her and introduced herself. "My name is Victoria Beaton. I'm here to see my father and I understand you might know where he is. Is he here?" she asked.

Emmy didn't say anything for a moment but her smile faded a bit as she took Victoria by the arm and guided her into the house. "You must be starving after your trip. Come in and sit down, I'll fix you a cup of tea and a sandwich."

Victoria was tired but the thought of seeing her father was greater. "Is he here Emmy?" she pressed.

Emmy came over to the table, sat down and took Victoria's hand. "Your father lived here many months; I knew him well. He was a kind man but a very sick man. I took care of him right up to the day he passed. That was over two months ago."

The words hit Victoria hard and she nearly fainted sitting there in the chair. Tears welled up in her eyes and her mouth was open in shock trying to understand what she had just heard. The realization was setting in that she had indeed lost both parents before she could get to them and it was unbearable.

She broke down sobbing in Emmy's arms and was inconsolable. Finally, Emmy's warm embrace and soothing tones brought Victoria back and she pulled away and tried to regain her composure.

Emmy told Victoria the story of how her father had come to Tucson from Tombstone looking to talk to a doctor and how he was told he was going to die. He came to her house to live out his final days in peace and comfort and told Emmy the story of how he had become a very rich man and that it was all for naught without the people he loved.

He told her about Millie and the decision he had made so long ago and the fact that he had a daughter who he had never seen.

Emmy told Victoria that Jim had sent her mother a telegram asking for her to please come but he never received an answer. He looked for a telegram every day, right up to the morning he died.

Victoria took the telegraph from her bag and told Emmy that Millie had never received it. She too had passed.

"How tragic," Emmy said quietly.

She showed Victoria to the room Jim had occupied up to his last day and told her she could stay as long as she wanted. She also showed Victoria a box containing her father's personal effects.

Victoria thanked the kind lady for looking after her father in such a loving way and told her that she would only stay a few days to get Jim's affairs in order and visit his final resting place. She was very tired and lay down to rest, falling into a deep sleep and dreaming about her lost parents.

She woke hours later to unpack and visit Emmy in the kitchen to continue their conversation and have dinner.

The next morning Emmy took Victoria to Jim's grave site and she was quite surprised to see how well it was being taken care of. Emmy told her that it was being looked after and tended every day. A bright white headstone had been placed so that you could read it from quite a distance away. It simply read: "Jim 'Bunny' Beaton, He Lies Here in Peace, 1827 – 1882."

Emmy told her that her father had donated a large sum of money to the church so his final resting place would always be looked after and they were happy to do it.

Victoria spent the majority of her time in Tucson at the gravesite and she buried a small locket that had belonged to her mother in front of the headstone so he would always have something of hers next to him.

She visited the doctor that had treated Jim and thanked him for helping her father in his final days. With that she was off to the bank.

She walked into the bank that sunny morning and met with the manager for over an hour. He offered his condolences for her loss and said that her father had been well-liked in Tucson. Victoria was told that Jim had amassed a large amount of money while he was in Tucson. That inheritance was now hers. The amount was well over a hundred thousand dollars and the manager asked her what she was going to do with such a sum.

Victoria advised the manager that he was to wire transfer the entire amount by Western Union to her bank in Chicago and confirm with her that it did arrive before she left town.

She had been in town about a week and was near completion of her business in readiness to leave and there was just one more thing to do. That was to go through the box with Jim's things and decide what she was going to take with her.

She sat on the bed, opened the box containing his old carpet bag and saddlebag and laid them on the bed. There wasn't much for a lifetime's worth of back-breaking work and breathing in the poisons that eventually took his life: an old top hat that had long been past repair, a pocket watch that had been broken long ago and stopped at 2:45, a piece of rock showing a small vein of silver running through it, a hand drawn map showing where the mine was located, a rough old harmonica that probably didn't hold a note, what looked like a medicine bag, probably given to him by an old medicine man, a flint and stone for making campfires, a pot for boiling coffee, a bedroll, a set of broken spurs, a pair of wire-framed glasses and an old gun belt with a broken peacemaker in it and a leather bag that contained a beautiful Colt 45 with a Walnut handle and scrolling up the barrel.

It wasn't much but to Victoria it was his world and she would treasure them forever. She wanted to leave something for Emmy but the possessions were too dear to her so she put $1,000 in an envelope, which she placed on the bed. Victoria knew that Emmy could use the money.

She went to the kitchen and said her goodbyes to the lady that had been with her father to his last day and told her that if she ever needed anything to cable her in Chicago immediately.

She walked out the front door at peace with herself, and didn't look back.

Her buggy stopped in front of the Wells Fargo Station and as Victoria was being helped down from the seat she noticed the Sheriff standing in his usual spot. She walked past him and heard him say "did you find what you wanted, Miss Beaton?"

Victoria stopped, turned her head and replied "yes I did Sheriff everything is going to be alright now." With that she entered the office to wait for the stage.

The stagecoach roared up to the office in a cloud of dust and curses came from the seat high in front of the coach. It was the Badger, looking like she had never been shot. She had on the same clothes, same Buffalo coat, same mule skinner hat and disposition.

"If you're coming, get in!" she screamed. "I don't have time to baby you wet-nosed dandies. I've got a schedule to keep."

Everybody piled in and before they could get properly seated, the Badger had already lit a fire under the team of horses by slapping her reins and cracking her long black bullwhip into the air.

The stagecoach disappeared in a cloud of dust.

Several days later Victoria made it back to Deadwood, visited her mother's grave one last time and left Jim's spectacles there with her just in front of the headstone. The circle was complete.

Chapter 31

Victoria spent some time with Belle while she awaited the train to Chicago. She also had time to think of all the things she had been through and the sadness of it all. It had been hard and she had to grow up quickly.

She wondered what she was going to do with herself now, being a governess was something she no longer wanted.

The train trip back would take several weeks and she would have plenty of time to think about her future.

There were several stops along the way to Chicago. People were getting on and off at different towns and cities along the way. The train itself needed water and coal to power the great engine's steam boiler.

She lost count as to how many stops the train made but found herself people watching to make the time go by quicker.

There were all kinds of train travelers, after all this was the late nineteenth century and the train was the transportation of the future. Young, old, large and small groups of people, families with children, salesmen and cowboys alike were using the train. There was even a group of real Plains Indians traveling in the next car. Everyone was discovering the train.

The stops in the towns were long enough for Victoria to get off and stretch her legs and even have something to eat. She even bought a basket in which she would purchase fresh fruit, cheese, bread and water to carry along with her when the stops were farther apart.

Victoria was a prolific reader. She loved books and how they could whisk her away to foreign lands or even chase a whale in the open ocean.

It was during one of these adventures she was having inside her current book that she met the person that would influence the rest of her life, Edwin Moses.

She hadn't really been paying attention to him but was aware that every time the train stopped he was the first off and the last on. He always brought something back with him and the pile around his seat was starting to get quite substantial.

He reminded Victoria of a Prairie Gopher popping in and out of a hole gathering nuts but he looked harmless so she forgot he was there.

One time during the trip, as she was sitting on a bench just outside the station waiting for some type of repair to be completed, she spotted him just around the train dragging a four foot wooden Indian up the stairs. She had no idea what he would want with it but he was going through a lot of trouble to get it into the car. She was going to have to ask him about it the next time she had an opportunity to speak to him.

On week three of the journey, Victoria was sitting by herself with her reading material on her lap. She loved to read all kinds of books and today it was Mobey Dick. She was so interested in what was going on in the book where the Captain of the ship was chasing a whale that she didn't see the little man come up and sit in the seat next to her.

Her head came up from her book and she looked directly at him. Before she had a chance to admonish him for being so rude, he said "pardon me Miss, I don't mean to intrude and I didn't mean to be so bold but I had noticed over the past weeks that you're traveling alone. So am I. I have, over time, noticed your reading material and admire the vastness of your choices. Mobey Dick is a classic, I must admit, but The Scarlet Letter and Madam Bovary, now that shows me a person that is not shy of reality. Oh, please, pardon me, allow me to introduce myself. My name is Edwin Moses, fellow traveler and a person starved for conversation, as I hope you are too."

Victoria was taken aback by the man's boldness at first but as she looked at him further, and from what she had seen of him during the trip, told her that he was indeed harmless and was only interested in trying to be friendly.

She smiled and extended her hand, "my name is Victoria Beaton and I'm traveling home to Chicago."

Edwin was taken aback for a second. "I'm heading for Chicago too," he said. "I live there also and run a small gallery of antiquities on the south side of the city.

"A gallery?" Victoria asked. "How interesting, please tell me more Mr. Moses."

That conversation struck up a friendship that would last over 20 years.

Edwin explained that he was exploring the mid-west United States for artifacts that he could show in his gallery and spent most of his time away. He was, as Victoria found out, hard to quiet down once he got talking about his work and was more than happy to show her what he had uncovered during his train trip across the country.

The more Edwin talked, the more interested Victoria was becoming and before the end of the journey, Edwin had little trouble convincing Victoria to tour his gallery after she was settled.

Chapter 32

A month after Victoria's return to Chicago she remembered Edwin's invitation and found herself in front of the Jessop Gallery of Antiquities, named after his late wife. Edwin met her at the front entrance and invited her to tour at her leisure and ask questions if she wanted.

The building was dated but well maintained. The displays and artifacts were well laid out but in Victoria's mind, there needed to be more. "More of everything," she thought.

Over the next few weeks Victoria visited the gallery often and she and Edwin would talk about his work and his passion for history.

It was becoming clear to Victoria that Edwin needed a partner and she wanted to be that partner. She put the question to him over tea one Tuesday afternoon and a half hour later they had become not only good friends but partners in the Jessop Gallery of Chicago.

With Victoria's input of capital and her love for the work, the Gallery's reputation of being a quality house improved greatly.

They were able to acquire better quality pieces without hunting for them and sales were steadily on the rise.

Her friendship with Edwin lasted right up to his passing some twenty years later. At the reading of his will Victoria found that Edwin had left her his half of the Gallery, making her the sole proprietor of the Jessop Gallery.

A short time after she had the Gallery renamed after her father, Jim Beaton. She thought it would be a great tribute to him and the old west.

As Victoria sat at Edwin's desk, now hers, and looked around at the business she had helped to build, she remembered how they had gotten together on that train so many years ago and the passing of her parents that put her on that train. It was so long ago.

She had put out her parents keepsakes on display some time back and had many offers from people to purchase them but they were not for sale. They were part of her past. There was just one more thing she had to do, the Colt 45.

She wanted the gun to remain in the gallery. It belonged there along with her father's other mementos, but she wanted it to be out of sight and secure. She had an old Irish carpenter build a false bottom in one of the drawers in the desk and that's where she placed Bunny's gun to remain for many years.

PART III

The Strange Partnership

Chapter 33

His hands were getting warmer, almost hot. He saw himself holding the gun with both hands and the room was spinning and melting away in front of him.

He could see Whitie sitting on the bench, dead, at the racetrack. He lifted his head and looked at Lou with dead eyes. "They killed me Lou," he said, then disappeared.

He saw himself in a foot race again, with mobsters shooting at him. A voice came out of nowhere, "you'll never find him flatfoot."

The room continued to spin. It was like being on a bad ride at an amusement park and your stomach tells you you're about to puke. He was scared to death and started screaming as his bed continued to spin more and his room changed shape around him.

A voice in his head was screaming "drop the gun, drop the gun." He saw himself slipping off the edge and falling into darkness.

His eyes snapped open and Lou found himself still clothed and about to fall off his bed, tied up in his only sheet. "A nightmare," he realized, "a nightmare that he would not soon forget."

The room had stopped spinning and he found himself in a sweaty mess and his breathing slowed.

The experience scared the hell out of him and the gun was on the floor. "What the hell had just happened?" he mumbled to himself as he looked down at his hand. At least it wasn't burnt.

Lou was a real mess that morning. He hadn't slept well all night from what he could figure. His eyes were red and bloodshot, he needed a shave and something must have crawled into his mouth and died. He needed to get out of his room and clear his mind.

He hadn't been through anything like that before and wasn't sure what to make of it. "Maybe he should lighten up on his alcohol consumption," he thought. He needed coffee real bad and something else in his stomach other than cheap whiskey.

He walked over to Maude's. The air would do him good. He settled into his booth to the smell of hot black nectar of the gods and fresh baking.

He was still deep in thought about what he experienced during the night and wasn't really catching anything that Maude was saying as she brought him a stack of pancakes, but he did pick up on the words "Whitie was here."

Lou came alive and gave Maude his full attention.

"Like I was saying, Lou," she continued. "Whitie was in here just last week and looked really worried. He didn't talk much, just sat in a booth and drank coffee. He looked real scared. I was watching him because the place was really quiet. There were just two other guys in the Diner, sitting in a booth beside him and they weren't ordering either, just talking."

Lou ate his breakfast and was starting to feel human again as he drank his second cup. He had an errand he had to run this morning, before he talked to Shamus about Whitie and there was no time like the present. He didn't like being shot at and if he was going to continue working as a private detective, he was going to have to even the playing field.

He needed to see Max Taylor, owner and proprietor of the Chicago East Gun Shop on East Roosevelt Road. Max had been in business for years and Lou knew him well from his police days.

Max would have what Lou was looking for. He climbed into his car, the 1934 Hudson T Coupe, and drove south on Michigan Avenue and was at the famous gun shop in twenty minutes.

He walked through the door and was not only greeted by a bear of a man coming over to him and just about breaking his hand as he said hello and "where have you been for so long," but his wife, Shirley, a lovely woman in her mid sixties, about 5'2, brown eyes and wore her graying hair pulled back.

They looked an odd pair to be running a gun shop but to people who knew them, it was no secret that Shirley was just as knowledgeable about every firearm in the shop and that she was deadly accurate with any one of them.

She gave Lou a hug and a punch in the arm. "Where have you been Lou Grimes?" she mused. "Stop being such a stranger, you're coming for dinner Friday night and that's the end of it." She disappeared into the back and they heard her putting on a pot of coffee.

"She's too good for you Max, you're a lucky man," Lou said.

"I know that, my friend," Max added. "I don't know how she puts up with me but we can talk more about that over dinner. What can I do for you?"

"I need some fire power Max, small and large," Lou said. "I'm looking for a handgun and a shotgun."

Max's face took on a questioning look. Lou went on to explain that he was in the "Private Detective" business now and he told Max about being shot at in the rail yard and losing his favorite hat. Max nodded his head, agreeing with his friend and told him to look around, take his time and have some of Shirley's coffee.

Max's shop was loaded to the doors with all kinds of post World War II weaponry from Ballester Molina A's and Berretta models 1934 semi-automatic handguns to shot guns and machine guns. Max had Tommy Guns and even 50 caliber, belt fed machine guns on tripods. He had everything. It was virtually a one-stop war zone.

It took a couple of hours and lots of questions for Max but Lou finally decided on what he needed; a Browning HP (FNGP 35 Belgium-made, 13 round semi-automatic handgun) that fit right into his hand and came with a shoulder holster and another Browning A5 Shotgun with a five round capacity (four in the mag and one in the chamber). It was light and fit well under Lou's trench coat, hanging from a leather strap. You would never know it was there and he liked that.

Lou couldn't get out of the shop unless he promised on his honor to come to dinner that Friday and Max crushed him with a friendly bear hug as he made his escape. He left the shop talking to himself, "good friends are hard to find."

You can't pack heat in Chicago without a permit so Lou drove down to the Police Station, paid his five dollars to make everything on the square and nice-like.

He met with Shamus at Eddie's that afternoon to go over what was happening in the Simms murder. There wasn't much to talk about. Whitie was indeed killed by a single stab wound to the liver in broad daylight at Palisades Park with not one witness and $25,000 was missing.

Lou showed Shamus his new toys and the permit so there would be no surprises down the line and Shamus agreed that Lou should be carrying all the time.

Shamus had to get back to work and Lou told him that he was going to dig around some, just to see what comes up.

He sat at the bar for another half hour, trying to piece things together and finally decided that he'd have to talk to Stella first. After all she was the last one to talk to Whitie and she was the one who gave him the money, just before he died.

He drove to the track and walked up to Saul's hotdog stand all smiles. He missed his favorite food and was about to make up for lost time and the gab that he and his friend would have during his feast.

"How's business you old miser?" Lou yelled over the crowd. He apologized for not being around the last couple of days. Whitie's murder was taking up all his time. Saul said business couldn't be better but things were really quiet on the street and if anyone knew anything, they weren't talking.

Lou thanked his friend and walked into the Palisades and up to Stella's window. "When is your break darlin?" he asked.

She looked up, recognized him, smiled and said "fifteen minutes Lou we can talk in the back."

Lou went back into the boss's office to wait for Stella and lit up his cigar again. Fifteen minutes later Stella came through the door and gave Lou a little hug before sitting down and looking over at him. "It's terrible Lou," she choked. "I still keep seeing him in front of me that day dumping all that money on my counter and the look on his face when I gave him "$25,000. Lou," she choked "I didn't even know that he was sitting there, dead until a lady screamed and the crowds started gathering around."

Lou reached over, took her hand and tried to calm her down. "I know it's rough Stella," he said, "but I need to know if you remember anything else since talking to the police."

"Nothing Lou," she sat back starting to calm down.

Lou took a second or two to take in what he was hearing and how it was affecting her. "Thanks Stella," he said, standing up and getting ready to leave. "If you think of anything else, you can call me at Eddie's."

He reached for the doorknob when Stella called to him, "Lou I don't know if this means anything, but when Whitie dumped that money on my counter he looked really relieved to get rid of it."

"Did you mention this to the Police?"

"No," she replied. "They just wanted to know how much he won and I didn't see anything out of the ordinary."

Lou thanked her again and left the office and the track with his head buzzing.

Chapter 34

It was the question of the day for Lou Grimes. Where did Whitie get all that money and a gun? Donavon wouldn't lend him another dime and the blood donor clinic wasn't paying that kind of dough.

He had come to the conclusion that the little weasel had indeed stolen it but from where and why wasn't it making noise on the street?

If it was mob money he would hear about it right away or maybe they wanted to catch the little rat first and save their reputation.

He spent the next day checking into all his favorite haunts and talking to street people that had their fingers on the pulse of the street: pool halls, off-track betting parlors and illegal poker games. He greased a lot of palms and if something had happened, he would eventually get word of it, money talks. The more you put out, the noisier it gets.

It was time to relax and do what he liked to do every day about this time. It was Eddie's. He walked right through the door and headed right to his stool. His feet were sore, his throat was dry and he had far more questions floating around his head than he wanted to right now.

Eddie dropped a cold beer in front of him along with a stack of notes. "What the hell is this shit, Eddie," he wanted to know.

"This is today's fan mail Lou," Eddie came back. "You're one popular P.I. these days. People want to talk to you about all kinds of jobs and Lou," Eddie said as he walked away, "I'm not you're answering service buddy, so you'd better figure it out."

He had about ten pieces of paper in front of him and as he sipped his beer he read them all and put them in two piles. One pile was people looking to hire him to follow somebody or some other crap and the other pile was people giving him the heads up or tips about possible things going down.

All this was valuable information down the line, but right now he was tired and it was only 11:00 PM. It was beer and bed for this old gumshoe but as he walked across the street and up the stairs to his room he noticed he was breaking out in a sweat. The gun, he knew he was going to try again tonight. He had to.

It was like holding an angry cat by the tail but he had to get to the bottom of it. If he couldn't, he could see only two other options, turn the gun over to Shamus or throw it in the river and get on with his life.

He walked into his room and had already decided that option two wasn't on the table yet, neither was option one. He went right to the drawer of the dresser and took the old gun out and put it on the bed. Tonight things were going to be different. He was going to be in control and take the horrible ride in stages.

He needed to confirm that it was indeed the gun that was causing all this turmoil so he took it out of the bag and put it on the bed. There was nothing. That was a good thing.

Next he picked it up and held it for a short time. It began to heat up so he dropped it on the bed again. Next time he held it longer before dropping it and it heated up again and the walls around his bed and room began to melt and move.

He started breathing deeper and dropped the gun one more time. "Well," he thought, "I'm still alive, so what the hell."

He grabbed the cat by the tail one more time. This time he held it for as long as his nerves would let him and his room was now taking on different moving colors as the walls continued to melt around him and a fog or mist formed at the foot of his bed. The mist swirled around and seemed to pull the walls toward him.

He was freaking out now but when blurred shapes began to form in the fog he lost his composure, dropped the gun and ran from his room across the street to Eddie's and downed three shots of Old Turkey before he could breathe again.

Eddie noticed that Lou was sweating heavily and looked like hell. Concerned for his friend, he went over to Lou and said "Lou you look like hell. What have you been doing? Do you need a doctor?"

Lou told Eddie that he was fine and just needed a couple more shots to calm his nerves. The whiskey started to settle him down so he tried to explain what was going on in his room with the walls melting and the mist and the colors. He left out the part about the gun.

Eddie started shaking his head and said "you gotta stop smoking that shit they smoke in Chinatown Lou and stick to your cigars."

Lou got a disgusted look on his face and said "thanks for the advice and the kind words buddy. I'll take it from here."

He made his way back to his room and the waiting gun. He was feeling no pain and his judgement was probably not what it should be but here he was, with the gun in his hand and a belly full of mind-numbing moonshine. He waited for what was coming, the heat, and the room melting around him, fog and haze forming and this time the floor seemed to have become an angry sea.

He was really having a hard time holding it together and could see the end of what was left of his courage when suddenly the gun cooled right down and so did the room, almost cold. As his eyes cleared, so did the fog and to Lou's utter terror, three figures stepped out of the fog and stood right in front of him.

He must have fainted or passed out because when he came to, he was on the floor, the gun beside him and the three specters he had seen the night before were gone.

Lou had a hard time convincing himself that he wasn't crazy and that he indeed had seen three forms at the foot of his bed the night before. It was a hard internal argument but he convinced himself that it was partly the booze, lack of sleep and who the hell knew what else.

He had to contact Shamus and find out if there were any noteworthy armed robberies or break-ins in the last week or so and get a list as to what was missing.

Shamus didn't get back to him until late in the afternoon. They sat around Lou's second office at Maude's and Shamus had brought with him three files.

"These are the latest and greatest my friend" Shamus smiled, "are you onto something that I should know about?" he asked.

"One or two things have come up," Lou offered "but nothing I can put my finger on. I'm just playing a hunch. You will be the first to know if they pan out."

They spent the next couple of hours going over the case files. One was a home invasion but the robber was shot to death trying to open a safe. Another was a small time bank job and the robber got away with $10,000 and a bullet in the back of his leg. "Looking at the amount of blood loss on the ground," Shamus said, "this guy wasn't long for this earth."

The third was a museum break-in. The old Beaton Museum over on East Street was broken into and the hoods made off with quite a haul of gold and silver coin collections along with jewelry and all kinds of other valuables.

"They broke the place up a bit doing it too. It was a surprise to me, seeing that there was a guard on duty," Shamus said. "Good thing he sleeps deep, he could have got hurt. They got away clean out the back door and into the night."

This file interested Lou and he asked Shamus if he could get a copy of the items that were missing from the old museum and a copy of the police report and he'd ask around.

They sat and talked late into the afternoon and said they would stay in touch if anything came up. Shamus would work his end of the robbery and Lou would work his. Shamus then got up to leave.

Lou had dinner before leaving Maude's and after giving her a big hug for such a great meal he went back to Eddie's for a liquid dessert and to be with his thoughts.

Eddie came up to him from the far side of the bar and commented. "You look better today than you did last night, you old bugger. Promise me you'll stay away from that shit," and he dropped a cold beer in front of him.

Lou shook his head and told Eddie that it must have been a bad dream, but he was better now.

Before leaving the bar, he told Eddie to keep his ears open and let him know if he heard any chatter from his customers about the museum heist. Eddie just nodded his head.

Chapter 35

Back in his room, Lou sat on his bed determined to get to the bottom of the matter of the gun, all the time keeping his 9mm Browning close by.

He picked up the old six-shooter and the ride began again. If you know what's coming and you've been there before, the experience isn't so scary but not knowing what comes after is.

That's where Lou was now. The fog and the mist was all around him and the shapes were beginning to form in front of him. Out of all the craziness stepped three men all dressed in black. They were over six feet tall and all had large mustaches, hats and six guns. "Cowboys?" Lou asked himself. They looked like cowboys but they also had the look of death about them and Lou immediately grabbed for his automatic thinking he was about to be bumped off by three street hoods that came out of nowhere.

The ghosts stood there, not making a move but their eyes were darting everywhere.

Lou went on the defensive immediately and demanded the man in front not move an inch. "How the hell did you get into my room?" he growled. "What the hell do you want here?"

The silence went on for some time until Lou finally yelled "who the hell are you?"

The man on the left moved forward and said. "You have five seconds to explain yourself before I kill you stranger."

Lou went for his gun in fear for his life. The man was much faster and the smoke and flame from his Frontier Peacemaker filled the air in front of him but didn't make any sound.

Astonished at this, he fired again. This time the man on the right stepped forward, backing up the first man and the same thing happened.

The cowboy in the middle went for his gun also but his holster was empty. He kept slapping the holster hoping to find what should have been there, but there was nothing.

The three gunmen looked at each other in disbelief, down at their weapons and finally back to Lou.

"What type of Injun black magic is this stranger?" The middle cowboy asked, "answer fast, I've got nothing for patience left and I'm about to crush you like a bug."

The man on the left was just behind him urging him on. "Get him, get him! Look at him he's nothing but a tin horn putting some kind of spell on us. Kill him!"

Lou stood his ground but still had the pistol and his own gun in his hand. He wanted to use it, but something wasn't making any sense. The men were right there in front of him but he was having trouble clearly focusing on them and the gun thing was scaring the shit out of him.

The cowboy in the centre of the three moved forward quickly with the intention of grabbing Lou's guns and punching him in the mouth at the same time. It was met with bitter disappointment and disbelief. His hand moved right through Lou's gun hand and his jaw! He was shocked beyond belief and stood back, looking at his hands.

After what seemed an eternity, the man on the left put his hand on the other's shoulder and faced Lou Grimes. "What is this place Mister and why are we here? What kind of Injun magic is this?"

Lou was just as shocked as the three cowboys were as to why they were in his little room. "How did you get here?" He didn't believe in ghosts and boogey men. All of this had to be a drug someone slipped into his beer. He was at a loss for words and found himself unable to speak until the man on the left moved forward again and reached out his hand to grab Lou's forearm and went right through it like Lou wasn't even there.

The ghost stepped back again and looked at Lou in disbelief. "Ok," he said, "let's try it another way tinhorn. My name is Virgil Earp. This is my brother Wyatt and my other brother Morgan. We are U.S. Marshalls from Tombstone, Arizona."

Today is Wednesday, 3:15 in the afternoon in the year 1881 and only a second ago we were in a gun fight at the O.K. Corral that created so much smoke, wind and dust I couldn't see or hear a thing but I know we were all wounded and when it all died down and the smoke cleared, we find ourselves in a place we've never been and not wounded."

The visitors were starting to get nervous as they realized that they were not in Tombstone anymore and a strange man in strange clothes was standing in front of them with a gun on them, two guns really.

Lou took a deep breath and started to explain things to his ghostly visitors that only now he was beginning to figure out. "My name is Lou Grimes, I'm a Private Investigator. You are in my room in a boarding house on the south side of

Chicago. It's 10 PM on Friday night and it's 1945. I have no idea what you three are doing here, but I want you to leave the way you came and don't come back."

Everybody started talking at once and nothing was making any sense. The Earp brothers were nervously walking around the small room and Lou was trying to follow them and get some answers.

The voices started getting louder and Lou heard a light knocking on his door. He didn't need any company at the moment so he'd have to get rid of them as quick as he could.

He hadn't quite gotten to the door when it opened wide and in walked Ruth. "What's going on here Mr. Grimes?" she asked. "Why are you yelling and stomping around so loudly? Mrs. Little, just below you is complaining that you're having a loud party. I can see you're by yourself so why are you carrying on so?"

Lou was shocked and so were the Earps. She couldn't see them, only Lou.

This didn't go by Morgan, the youngest and he walked right up to her and put his hand through Ruth's head. "Stop that right now and get away from her," Lou scolded. Morgan was laughing loudly but Ruth was horror struck at the way Lou was talking to her. "Well I never!" she yelled back and left the room, slamming the door behind her.

"She couldn't see them or hear them, why?" Lou asked himself. With all that was happening he was suddenly tired and had to sit down at his little table. As he did so, he put the guns on the table.

This didn't go unnoticed and in a split second Wyatt was launching himself from across the room at Lou and the two guns. "My gun!" he yelled "my gun! Where did you get your hands on my gun? Give it back to me right now Mister, or I'm going to kill you as sure as there is a hell."

Lou was getting used to not being touched and he did see with his own eyes, when Morgan put his hand through Ruth's head but he was really surprised that Wyatt recognized the old pistol.

Wyatt reached for the gun and his hand passed right through it and the table.

The other two brothers came over and looked down at the pistol as Wyatt steadied himself and turned around and screamed "Injun black magic," and began pounding his head with his fists.

Virgil, being more sensible asked Lou in a calm voice "where did you get that shooting iron tinhorn?"

Lou was getting a little ticked off being called a tinhorn one too many times and got up to look Virgil in the face.

"I'm going to tell you again Earp, my name is Lou Grimes and I'm a Private Investigator."

Morgan came up behind Virgil and began yelling at him "you're a Pinkerton man, aren't you?" as he spat on the floor.

Lou told him that there was indeed a Pinkerton Agency in town but he wasn't one of them. His job was to look for people that had broken the law and turn them into the police when he found them and for that he got paid.

Wyatt came back to the table and looked down at his gun that was so close and yet so far away. He looked up from his gun and once again at Lou. "You're a miserable bounty hunter aren't you?" he said.

Wyatt told Lou that he had lost his gun right after the gun fight because it had been shot out of his hand and with all the sand and dust couldn't find it. He went back hours later to no avail. The gun was gone. Now here it was. "How did my gun get to Chicago 64 years later in 1945?" Wyatt asked.

Lou had no answers, but he explained to his visitors how he had come into possession of Wyatt's beloved six-shooter. He told them about the track, crazy Whitie and how Lou had bought the gun from him only to find that he had been murdered shortly after.

Lou had no answers about the questions the visitors were asking but he was going to find out.

It was really late, 2 AM and Lou had a feeling that it was about to get real busy around his little world in the morning.

"I'm going to bed now," he said. "I don't know how you ghosts do it but I'm climbing into that bed over there and closing my eyes."

He turned and put the revolver into the drawer and was about to tell them to get the hell out of his room but found that he was already alone. They had disappeared. His head hit the pillow and he mumbled "ghosts, guns; Christ what a day!"

Chapter 36

The next morning Lou rose early so he could go downstairs and apologize to old Mrs. Little. Then he came back to his room to boil a pot of coffee and burn a piece of toast on his hotplate. It was going to be a long day.

He sat at his little table and replayed the night before in his head. He realized it wasn't a bad dream. His room fell apart on him and he did have a visit from three ghosts, cowboys no less, "the goddamn Earp Brothers for god's sake."

It was like a book Lou had read in school many years before about a guy who had been visited by three ghosts at Christmas time. He didn't remember much about the storey; only that it made for a long night for the old man and in the end, everybody ate turkey.

He recalled talking to Virgil about how they had got to his room after the gunfight and how Wyatt reacted when he saw the old pistol on the table. "Could it really be his gun?"

he thought. "How could he prove that the old pistol belonged to a famous old gunfighter? If it were true, how did Whitie get Wyatt Earp's gun?"

Finding out whether or not Lou's old gun had indeed once been owned by the famous lawman should be easy he thought. After all it was part of history. He would spend the better part of the day at the public library and do some research on the Earps. He wanted to get a few things straight in his mind before his next conversation with his unwanted guests.

Lou stepped out of his building and went across the street to Eddie's to check in and pick up his messages. He had to cut a deal with his friend to take them. For that Eddie would receive a couple of bucks at the end of every week. He also wanted to see if Eddie had heard anything from any of his customers.

He was in a hurry to get downtown so he just collected his messages, which were substantial and stuffed them in his coat pocket.

Eddie told him he wasn't hearing anything but he should stop by later just to catch up.

Lou drove downtown to a huge brick building that had been there since the city was founded and went through the doors of the Library to be dwarfed by tall towering shelves that contained thousands of books and archives.

He was out of his element here so he asked one of the ladies that worked there to show him where he could find things "western" and in particular Tombstone and the Earp brothers.

She kept leading him deeper into the labyrinth of twisting rows upon rows of books turning this way and that until finally they came to an area called "Western Action Adventure History." Lou shook his head. This is where he needed to be.

Before the lady left he made a crack about, if he wasn't out by the end of the day to come and find him. He thought it was funny but the lady didn't. "So much for his charm," he thought.

His first search was for information on Wyatt Earp himself and his exploits in the Wild West leading to Tombstone and the gun fight at the O.K. Corral.

All Wyatt's facts about the fight were there including an article about his famous gun going missing and was still missing to date. The gun was well described and documented to be a Bluntline Colt 45 with a 12 inch scrolled barrel and walnut handle bearing the serial number 33909. It was one of only four ever made, a true western mystery as to its whereabouts.

Lou spent hours in amongst the books, manuscripts and copies of marriage and death certificates and came away stunned and shocked at what he had uncovered. He, Lou Grimes was related to the Earp clan in a distant way by way of Lou's father's father, living in a small town called "Biggsville" Illinois, just a short distance from where Wyatt's parents were living in Monmouth, Illinois before moving to California to be farmers.

Wyatt's father, Nicholas married twice and had ten children, five of them boys and sometime between 1825 and 1898 the Earps and the Grimes family came together on the western frontier and Lou found himself to be a distant cousin in the Earp lineage on his mother's side. "And what about that curse?"

That was it, Lou's head was reeling and he had to get out of the building. He almost ran into the librarian. His head was spinning and he just about crashed his car into a pole, thinking about what he had discovered on his way back to Eddie's. He needed a beer!

He walked into the bar and sat down on his stool with a thump. Eddie noticed this and asked if he was okay. Lou came back with the only thing he could think of. "Just saw a ghost Eddie, just saw a ghost. Can you get me a sandwich and get me drunk, buddy. It's been one hell of a day."

Before heading back to his room the phone rang one more time. It was Shamus. "I was looking for you today Lou, where did you get off to?" he asked.

"You wouldn't believe me even if I told you," Lou came back.

Shamus said "let's get together tomorrow so I can give you copies of the two files you wanted, the police report and the insurance claim on the items missing from the robbery."

Lou thanked his friend and promised to get together with him at Maude's at lunchtime and go over the files.

With that and the beer buzz he was experiencing, it was time for the rack. It really had been a long day and he didn't want to play Mr. Scrooge tonight.

He woke the next morning with a hazy head and with that bad taste in his mouth again that only coffee would cure. His coffee could kill or cure so he was hoping on the latter as the smell of the black nectar assaulted his nose.

He had made detailed notes of the documents he had found in the library the day before and had drawn a picture of Wyatt's gun. It looked like a match but he was going to have to do better than that before Lou would believe him.

He looked out the window to the street below while sipping his coffee and remembered that he had told Benny a couple of days prior that he would look in on him. Today he was going to do just that.

He would deal with the Earps later but something inside him was telling him to visit Benny.

He went downstairs to the main door and the street but he stopped at the front desk. Ruth was looking over some paperwork and did not see him until he called her name. "Ruth," he said. She looked up, startled. "I didn't know you had a key to my room."

She looked at him sheepishly. "Change the lock today!" he demanded "and the damn light bulb."

"If I catch you in there again, I'll call the police and move out. Is that clear, Ruth?" he was looking right at her. She nodded and went back to her paperwork as Lou stepped out into the street.

It was a pleasant walk up the street to the corner and Benny's newsstand. He was looking forward to it but not what he found when he got there. He looked into the newsstand to find his friend sitting in the corner like normal but things were drastically different. Benny had been mugged and beaten badly. He explained to Lou that it had happened two nights ago by thugs that not only wanted his money but wanted to give him a message. He was to mind his own business and keep his mouth shut about what was going on in the neighborhood. The thugs had heard that Benny was chirping out to people that didn't need to know their business and they had been sent there to educate him or worse.

Benny had a black eye, bruises around his cheek and lower lip, along with it being split badly and was horribly swollen. He told them he got the message so they would leave but he still reached out to Lou for help.

Lou told his friend he was going to have Shamus make sure there were more patrols around the newsstand from then on and he put his arms around Benny's shoulders. "They're going to pay for this Benny, I promise."

Benny was really scared, "they t-t-t-told me n-n-not to s-s-say anything or th-they'd b-be b-back, b-but Lou," his frightened friend said, "I'm s-sure they w-were the s-same g-guys th-that are r-r-robbing and b-b-b-beating p-p-people in the neighborhood. D-didn't s-s-see the d-d-driver b-b-but the t-two m-m-monkeys w-were t-t-t-tall. One b-b-bald, the other had a b-b-big b-b-black b-b-b-beard."

Lou stayed with Benny the rest of the morning and promised to stop by near the end of the day. Inside he was raging. He was going to kill the rats. They needed killing.

He was still angry as hell as he entered Maude's to find Shamus already having coffee. "I was beginning to think you stood me up," he said as Lou sat down in the booth. "I thought we'd have some lunch before going over the files." Shamus noticed the angry look on his friend's face, "what's up Lou?" He was genuinely concerned.

Lou told him everything that he had just learned from Benny and had Shamus promise to have a patrol go by Benny's stand as much as possible. He also told Shamus that Benny was sure they were the same two pukes that were working his neighborhood and he was going to find them and make them pay.

Shamus reminded him that it was police business but deep inside he knew that he was going to have to find these guys before Lou did.

Lunch was good as always and a big piece of homemade apple pie brought them around to the files.

Lou looked at lists and lists of gold and silver coins that were worth vast amounts of money, along with necklaces, bracelets, gold goblets and rare Indian artifacts from the old west; things like a set of silver spurs and a badge that was said to be worn by Bat Masterson himself as well as memorabilia from the great gold and silver strikes in early western United States. There was a small handpick with a silver striker, a beat up old scale, a flint striker, a harmonica and a time piece from a miner long dead. They had even taken a piece of rock that had a silver streak running through it.

One thing stood out for sure for both Shamus and Lou, the thieves had time to go through the place and the old guard slept like the dead.

The investigative report showed that the thieves came in from the back door and made their way through the gallery, breaking display cases or defeating locks. They even destroyed an old desk that was in the corner for some reason. The drawers were empty and had been smashed by an old wooden Indian arm that had been broken off to use as a hammer.

They talked about the files for quite some time and Shamus asked Lou if he was getting any information on the street. Nobody was talking.

Shamus got up to leave and told Lou he was going over to talk to Benny and assure him that his friends would be watching from now on.

Lou took the files and drove back to Eddie's bar to sit and look over the lists again. After two cold ones and a shot of Old Turkey he had come to the realization that this much stolen stuff couldn't stay hidden for long.

He then decided it was time to go back to his room and finish up with his unwanted guests. He would tell them to take a hike and leave him alone, even if he was their cousin because relatives are a pain in the ass.

Lou walked into the brownstone, stopped at Ruth's desk and before he could ask, she handed over a key to his new lock. He climbed the stairs and entered his room with his files and looked around to see if anything was out of place. Once he was satisfied that all looked well, he went to the drawer and removed the bag with the pistol in it and went to his little table.

It was time to get this party started so he picked up the old pistol and went through a shorter version of what he knew was coming.

Out of the fog, the Earp brothers emerged.

"What did you find out about my gun tinhorn," Wyatt spat as he emerged from the fog and came right up to Lou with a menacing look on his face.

Lou ignored him, which made Wyatt even angrier and began talking to Virgil. "I've got a few ideas as to how this gun got into the hands of a crazy asshole like Whitie Simms but there's still a lot to dig up before I can say for sure."

Virgil was shaking his head in agreement and asked if there was anything that they could possibly do to help him.

While all this was going on Morgan was trying to agree with Wyatt, that Lou had disrespected him and needed his ass kicked.

Lou sat down on his chair and looked at the three lawmen. "Well, he finally said I think I know why you're here."

This got the cowboys' attention and all three got very quiet, fixing their attention on the detective.

"First," Lou said, "I have to confirm that this old Colt is indeed Wyatt's gun."

"Of course it is!" Wyatt said. "Just look at it, that's my gun," he continued. "It's a Bluntline Colt 45 Special, only four ever made."

Lou was ready to test him. "Okay Wyatt," he said. "What's the serial number?"

Wyatt smiled back at him and said "33909 tinhorn."

Virgil was watching them quietly and finally spoke up. "There's only one way to put an end to this guessing Wyatt, and you know what it is."

Wyatt smiled again. "If that isn't my gun," he went on, "then you won't find my initials under the walnut grip and we can put an end to this shit."

Lou was caught by surprise by this statement. This wasn't in the archives that he had looked at. Without further conversation, he stood up and went to a small toolbox he kept under his bed. He put the gun down on the table and found the setscrew that was holding the walnut grip to the weapon and began loosening it off.

At first it was difficult and Lou thought he might strip the old screw but eventually it gave way and began to spin out of the hole. The screw fell away and Lou sat there looking at the handle.

"Go on tinhorn," Wyatt teased. "Take a look under that grip and tell me what you see."

The ghosts came closer as Lou lifted the handle grip, turned it over and put it on the table. There in plain sight, carved into the walnut were the initials "W.B.S.E."

Wyatt stood up straight and put his hand down to his empty holster. "Told you she was mine," he said. "I burned my initials in there with a red hot horseshoe nail soon after I got it. How in the hell did you get here?" he said quietly, looking at what he loved the most.

"Okay," Lou said "we have confirmed that this gun is indeed Wyatt Earp's."

Lou sat back down and poured himself a drink. "I'm sorry I can't offer you any to celebrate but you know how it goes. This next little bit of information I dug up is going to knock you on your asses, if that's possible."

Before Lou could continue, Morgan tilted his head and drew his pistol. "There's someone in the hall, I feel it," he said. He stepped away from the group and walked to the door stepping through it like it wasn't even there.

A moment later he came back into the room and holstered his 45. "If I could have shot her, I would have," Morgan said. "It's the old woman who runs this shit hole. She's walking down the hallway, but I'm sure she was listening at the door."

"Doesn't matter right now," Lou said. "She can only hear and see me, not you guys. She must think I'm going nuts. Anyway," Lou said, "I have, I think the reason you guys keep coming to me. I did a lot of digging through the archives along with birth and death certificates from several of your ancestors and mine that could be found. It would seem that our families lived quite close to one another around a hundred years ago. You're grandfather, Nicholas Porter Earp married twice and had ten kids, five of them were boys and they all grew up around Monmouth, Illinois which is about 250 miles from here. My grandfather and his family lived in Bigsville just 12 miles away and had a large family of his own. The records get sketchy around that time period but I managed to pull some of them together and found that after all that coming and going between the families, marrying and dying, my name shows up as a distant cousin on my mother's side."

There was nothing but silence then Wyatt got that deadly stare in his eyes. "You're lying tinhorn," he said "if I could shoot you, you'd already be dead. You're a tinhorn lying dog."

It took many hours to convince the Earps that Lou was really their long lost cousin. He had made notes of all the material and documents he could and the brothers went over every last piece of it.

They had lots of questions and argued amongst themselves most of the time but the facts were the facts. Virgil had always been the most logical of the brothers and he eventually came to the realization that it could be true, maybe.

Morgan kept saying "well I'll be, well I'll be. Who'd a thunk it," as he looked at the paperwork.

The brothers talked and talked and Lou tried to fill in the blanks as they came up and then there was silence. It was like someone had turned down the volume on the radio and the room was filled with silence or was it acceptance.

The three brothers exhausted all the reasons why Lou couldn't be their cousin and were coming to terms with the idea that he could but that didn't answer the big questions they still had. "Why was the gun here and why were the brothers here?"

Lou poured himself another rather large glass of whiskey and made sure Wyatt saw how much he was enjoying it. "You're an asshole, cousin," he said.

"I agree, cousin," he replied, "I'm an asshole, but at least I have told you everything I know. You on the other hand have been holding back, haven't you Wyatt? You haven't told us about the curse."

"What curse," Virgil demanded. "What the hell is he talking about Wyatt?"

"What's this about a curse Wyatt?" Morgan choked, a little shaken.

"It's a matter of public record, you might want to look it up," Lou went on. "It seems that my cousin here, in his younger days, just prior to arriving in Tombstone had been tracking a band of Sioux warriors for many days and weeks. The Sioux had moved deeper into Indian Territory and camped near the Snake River. Wyatt's little band of Indian hunters found the settlement and raided the encampment in the middle of the night. Many Indians and white men died that night along with women and children. Wyatt's horse was shot out from underneath him as he was charging through the camp firing at anything that moved. Unfortunately during that raid the Chief's only son and the Medicine Man's daughter were killed. According to witnesses of the shooting, Wyatt and another man, Bart Knowles were found responsible for both deaths and were to be tortured and burned alive.

The Medicine Man, Blackcrow, was mad out of his mind with grief and called upon the devil himself to put a curse on Wyatt and his ancestors to rise from the dead as spirits and serve the ancestors of the gun that killed his daughter whenever it called. The gun was evil and the curse was to continue until the Earp line was no more.

Moments later, according to the report the posse charged the camp again freeing Wyatt and retrieving his gun. Knowles got away and was never heard from again."

"What the hell is he talking about Wyatt?" the brothers wanted to know.

"It didn't go down that way at all," Wyatt replied.

"History says it did," Lou said and produced a document he copied detailing the massacre at the Snake River settlement by a man named Bartholomew Knowles."

"Knowles was a bald faced liar! He made up the story," Wyatt howled as the brothers pored over the document.

"It was just a bunch of crazy savages and a screaming Medicine Man running around the camp, holding my gun in the flames," he said.

Morgan was really angry and began poking Wyatt in the chest. "Well something happened big brother," he said. "Because here we are and over there," pointing at Lou "a brand new cousin."

Lou had to admit it was a great story. "Awe, will you look at that, our first family fight." He looked at his watch, it was 2 in the morning and he was done with all the drama. "Get out of here," he said. "We'll pick this up in the morning."

He didn't even look back at the ghosts. He just put the gun away and knew they were gone.

Chapter 37

Lou spent a sleepless night tossing and turning, unable to get the ghosts out of his head and what he had uncovered. "What was he going to do with three ghosts from the 1800's who were obviously not going to go away?"

He dragged himself out of bed the next morning and sat at the foot trying to wake up. Suddenly to his left he heard a voice. "You look like shit in the morning Lou."

The voice startled him and he grabbed for his gun. "That's not a friendly thing to do cousin," Virgil said.

Lou looked closer and found the ghosts standing in his room, waiting for him to wake up. "Don't you guys ever sleep?" he asked. He caught himself in mid-sentence. "Sorry about that, what are you doing here? I didn't call you and the gun is still in the drawer."

Virgil came over to the bed and looked down at him. "We know why we're here. It's the gun. But as long as it is here and you are here, we'll come and go as we please. Besides we have a few questions of our own that need answering and you being a detective are going to help us answer them."

"You're out of your minds, if you have them," Lou replied. "I'm a busy man, I've got things to do and places to go and a killer to catch."

He then noticed that the ghosts seemed much clearer to him today, almost real.

Wyatt came over to him and said "you may be busy but we've got things that we need you to do, questions we need answered like how did that gun get here and who killed Morgan that night in the saloon while me and him were playing pool."

Lou had to admit that the gun was part of his investigation, but the killing of Morgan Earp was another story that was going to take some doing to solve.

Lou thought as he got dressed, "how in the hell was he going to drag these three ghosts along with him when he wasn't even sure they could leave the room."

Maybe just maybe he had a plan. "You guys can do the walk through the walls thing, right? You can hear things I can't." The three nodded. "Three more sets of eyes are better than just two and besides, you're old time lawmen but nevertheless still lawmen, and you can still sense when something isn't right and can tell me when I can't see it." They all agreed.

"Do what I ask you and keep a sharp look out for shit that might come my way."

Lou and his new posse of detectives stepped out of the room and went down the stairs. They walked by Ruth at the desk, and Virgil told Lou "she thinks you're an asshole cousin and can hardly wait for you to move out."

"You can read her thoughts?" Lou asked.

"Sometimes, but not always," Virgil replied.

"Then you can read my thoughts and I don't have to be talking out loud to you and maybe make people think I'm going crazy?"

Virgil just nodded.

They stepped out onto the street for the first time, the ghosts stopped and stepped back, not ready for what they were seeing.

There wasn't a horse anywhere to be seen. Black machines of some type were moving up and down the street. Buildings were made of stone, not wood. Small trains were moving down the middle of the street with no steam coming from the roofs. The noise and the people overwhelmed the ghosts at first but Lou calmed them down and told them to relax and watch. There would be plenty of time for questions later on.

He had to get to Maude's to have breakfast. It was a habit he was getting used to.

He stopped at his car and was about to get in when he noticed the ghosts standing back. "Come on he said, get in."

"What the hell is that?" Wyatt asked.

"It's a car," Lou explained. "It's what we get around in these days. It's much faster than a horse and more comfortable than a saddle."

The brothers got in reluctantly and held on for dear life as Lou started up the engine and sped out.

"Holy shit, how do you stop this thing?" Morgan yelled.

"Don't worry so much," Lou told him. "Just relax and look around at what has happened since you died."

It took only a few minutes for the cowboys to get used to traveling faster than they ever had before. They drove past the tallest building they had ever seen. A fire truck then went by with sirens blasting and would have killed the brothers right there if they hadn't already been dead.

They got to Maude's and stopped in the parking lot. The Earps got out of their first car ride breathing heavily with eyes wide open. "That was incredible," Wyatt said.

"If you think that was wild wait until you see what the rest of the day is going to be like," Lou offered.

They walked into Maude's and sat in his favorite booth. The ghosts were surprised to see that the train car they walked into was actually a place to eat.

The four were seated in Lou's booth but to anyone looking, they could only see Lou talking to himself.

Maude came over and gave him a big hug and asked him where he had been. "You know how it goes these days Maude, you just get busy."

She poured his coffee and a minute or two later came back with bacon and eggs, toast and more coffee. "You guys are really missing a treat," Lou said. "This is the best place in town to eat."

"I might not be able to eat," Morgan said but I sure can smell the hell out of it."

"You can go sit in the car if this bother's you, cousin," Lou jabbed.

He finished his breakfast and took out the files he was reading the night before. This got the brothers' attention and they were all ears when Lou began explaining about the robbery and how there might be a link to Whitie and the gun.

He didn't see Maude come up behind him, but she saw that he was talking to himself and got concerned.

"You okay Lou?" she asked.

"Yeah, I'm okay Maude," he replied. "Just not getting enough sleep lately." Maude shook her head and walked away.

Lou went on to explain to the cousins that a lot of loot was missing from the museum and these were the lists of missing stuff and the damages.

The ghosts were all over the papers and were talking to each other at great lengths before looking back at Lou. "What's up next Lou," Virgil asked. "We're with you."

"Well," Lou said, "we've still got half the day left so we better hit the bricks and start asking questions." He looked at the ghosts "now you're going to see and listen to some of Chicago's most interesting citizens lie right to your face so keep your eyes and ears open so we don't get into any trouble we can't get out of."

The lawmen got back in the car and drove across town to Lou's favorite old haunts, Barnaby's Row, better known as Skid Row.

Lou started on one side of the street and walked down to the train tracks talking to prostitutes and bag ladies alike. Everyone had something to sell but the Earps could sense that it wasn't what Lou was looking for and told him to save his money.

Pool Halls and Poker games alike, nobody knew anything or they just weren't talking. Virgil could tell when someone was lying. All they could do was move on.

They neared the end of the block, and Virgil told Lou to stop for a minute. He sensed something wasn't right and moved forward along with Wyatt, down the sidewalk to look down an alleyway that was just to their left. They walked into the alley and a second later, back out.

They went back to Lou and told him that there was a very big man with a very big bat just around the corner waiting for him. Lou figured something was up. The street was just too quiet. He nodded his head and took out his 9mm and Blackjack. He moved to the corner of the alley with his gun at the ready and he made more noise than he would have, causing the hidden man to rush out with the bat high above his head and stopped in his tracks.

He was looking down the barrel of Lou's brand new Browning. "Drop the bat pretty boy and tell me why you wanted to bash my head in."

The man dropped the bat and stood up to look at Lou in the face. "Talk you monkey," Lou growled.

The unknown man began. "Word on the street is that you're nosing around into things you shouldn't and people will pay good dough to shut you up."

"What people," Lou growled as he slapped the man's face.

"Don't know who they are," the man yelped.

Lou let him go. "Go to these people you don't know and tell them I'm not stopping and if they want to talk to me, I'm not hard to find."

The man ran down the alleyway and Lou and the Earps continued on.

No one was throwing around any new money or talking about the robbery but they knew and so did the Earps that sometimes you just can't beat it out of a guy. Wyatt wanted to do just that. Lou reminded him that murder was still a capital offense and they still hung people for it.

The pawn shops and loan sharks hadn't heard of the stuff moving but it was only a matter of time.

People were avoiding Lou and left the street when they saw him coming. He was sure they had been told to stay away from him but not all people do what they're told.

Alice Skrantz was an old friend and one of these people. She told Lou that the word on the street was to keep their mouths shut or someone would shut it for them.

Lou and the ghosts walked back to his car and got in. "What a waste of time that was," said Virgil.

"There are a lot of scared people around here Lou" Morgan said.

"Not entirely boys," Lou smiled. "We got under someone's skin with all that poking around and it could be only one person, Donavon. Let's call it a day guys and pick it up tomorrow," Lou offered. "I need a beer and a sandwich and a friendly face."

He drove over to his building and parked the car. "You guys can take the rest of the night off or follow me over to my bar and watch me drink in front of you, your call," Lou said.

"A saloon, a real saloon?" Wyatt asked. "They still have saloons?"

"Of course we do," Lou replied. "We're not heathens."

"Lead me to it cousin," Virgil added.

With that, Lou and his ghostly posse crossed the street and walked into Eddie's.

They went through the door and the ghosts were introduced to a 40's neighborhood bar, complete with pool tables and card games. The place was well-lit but lacked that smell of horse and stale men. It was not as loud as the Orient in Tombstone because no one was playing the piano.

"Well," Wyatt said out loud, "at least the whores are still the same."

They were just ladies that had come in with their men and not saloon whores like Wyatt had thought, but who was he to burst his bubble.

"Well at least there's a bar," Virgil said slapping his hand down and going through it.

Eddie brought Lou a beer and the Earps watched him as he greedily downed the glass and burped. Lou could see that he was getting to them but he wasn't sorry, he did warn them.

"You're a greedy bastard cousin," Wyatt said and with that they were gone.

"Thank Christ for that," Lou said to himself and fished around in his coat pocket for a piece of old cigar. To find his old stogie he had to pull out many pieces of paper that Eddie had written messages on. "I should read these," he thought "just to be sure I'm not missing a job of a lifetime."

He smiled to himself again. It was good to be wanted.

He read through the messages and noted one person had been trying to get in touch with him three times. It was an Old Italian Lou knew named Jimmy Sepitellie who had a sausage and butcher shop over on the corner of Dearborne and Madison. "Need to see you Lou, just as soon as you get this message. It's very important."

Lou had known Jimmy for a long time. He had the best pepperoni in Chicago and he would definitely be there first thing in the morning.

He checked his room every time he returned now. He didn't trust Ruth anymore and when things settled down he was going to be looking for a new place. For now, it was lights out and bring on another day.

"Maybe the Earps would take the day off," he thought "and leave him alone for once."

No such luck. Lou woke to find them waiting for him to come alive so they could get moving.

"Never seen anybody that needed so much sleep," Morgan said. "Half the day is gone and he hasn't even got his britches on yet!" It was 6 AM.

Chapter 38

Lou resigned himself to the fact that these cousins of his were going to be around for the long count so he was going to have to put them to work.

He made coffee and they talked about what had happened the day before and he showed them the piece of paper with Jimmy's message on it. "What do you think it means?" Virgil asked.

"Don't really know," Lou said as he drank his coffee, "but if Jimmy is asking me to come and see him, it's got to be something."

They pulled up to Jimmy's shop at 7:30 in the morning and had to wait for him to open. That was a mistake on Lou's part. He bought a newspaper and tried to read it. The ghosts were all over it, asking questions about everything that was happening in Chicago. Lou gave up and just let them have the damn thing.

At 8 o'clock Jimmy opened his door and was surprised to see his friend standing there waiting for him. "I've been calling and calling," Jimmy said.

It was too early in the morning for Jimmy to be waving his hands around in the air so it must be important. Jimmy's excitement always brought the Italian out in him. "I've seen them Lou, I've seen them." Jimmy was grabbing Lou by the coat.

"Seen who Jimmy?" Lou wanted to know.

"The bad men Lou, the bad men you've been looking for. That everyone is looking for," he yelled excitedly.

The ghosts spread out and began looking around, making sure Jimmy did not have any unwelcome guests. When they came back to Lou, Wyatt shook his head. Jimmy was still going on, waving his hands in the air, "two days ago Lou, two days ago and then one day ago too."

Lou was listening intently. "Where did you see them my friend? Calm down and tell me."

"Right across the street," he said. Lou looked to see where his friend was pointing City Billiard Hall of Chicago came into view. "These are bad men Lou," Jimmy said. "I have heard how they beat up and rob our friends. Make them go away please!" Jimmy was shaking.

Lou calmed him down and reminded him that these men did not know they had been identified so he was safe. The pool hall would soon be open, Jimmy told his friend.

Lou said he would hang around his shop and watch across the street to see if the men showed up. Jimmy's wife made sure that Lou was well fed and the coffee never ended.

Around noon, while Lou was sitting in a chair near the window and his partners were reading an opened newspaper on the table a black sedan rolled up to the pool hall and Benny Smalls got out of the car. He must have thought he was pretty safe because he didn't even look around.

"He's here," Lou said and the whole room came alive. He turned to Jimmy and told him to wait ten minutes then phone the police and ask for Sergeant Shamus O'Hearn, tell him what was happening and to bring the cavalry.

Lou stepped into the street and looked around making sure that Frank Crown was nowhere to be seen. He told the Earps to go into the pool hall and make sure that Benny was alone and that there were no other surprises waiting for him. They were gone in a second and Lou checked his 9mm and cocked a shell into his hidden shotgun.

He waited by the door for his partners to return and looked over to see Jimmy watching from his door. He waved him back inside as the Earps returned and told him that Benny was indeed alone playing pool but he had a gun.

The ghosts disappeared again into the pool hall. Lou moved quietly into the building and up the stairs to a very large pool room. He found one of the Earps just outside the door, it was Virgil. "He's to the left about 20 feet with his back to you right now," Virgil said.

Lou was just about to enter the room and confront Benny when Wyatt came into view and told him that a second man was in another room pissing up against the wall and he had a gun also.

He had to move fast and use the Earps to alert him to the man in the bathroom. He kicked open the door to the pool hall and leveled the pistol on Benny yelling at him not to move. Benny froze in mid-stroke and stood up, not showing Lou his face and one arm.

Lou was getting excited over Benny's refusal to obey his commands and was about to move forward to push him onto the pool table so he could reach for the gun. From his right side Wyatt yelled at him to get down just as a bullet whizzed past his ear and dug itself into the doorway. Another round was coming his way, only this time Lou was ready for it and moved to his left as it sped by.

Now it was his turn. He had to eliminate the threat quickly and the best way to do that was the pump shotgun. He pulled the trigger and the weapon came to life and cut the man in half. This moment of gunfire and action was just enough time for Benny to crouch down and get to the doorway before Lou could react to him.

He was taking the stairs two at a time but Morgan had no trouble following him down and out the door into the street. Benny moved forward with his gun in his hand to die seconds later in a hail of gunfire from the police waiting outside.

For a moment Morgan forgot himself and grabbed his pistol to return fire before he came to his senses. "Jesus Lou," he said, "I thought I was dead. Then I remembered I was," and he chuckled.

Lou came out into the street to be met by Shamus and around twenty policemen. "You said to bring the cavalry," Shamus said, "I didn't know what that meant. So this is what I brought."

Lou looked at his friend and nodded toward the pool hall. "There's another guy upstairs," Lou said that didn't want to surrender either, just to let you know." Shamus nodded quietly and sent a half a dozen officers up the stairs.

"We only got one Shamus," Lou said. "Frank Crown is still out there, and he's probably watching us right now."

It wasn't far from the truth. Frank Crown was indeed watching what was going on and saw his friend gunned down in the street. It was only Frank's common sense that kept him from running out into the street with his gun in his hand to shoot as many of these pigs as he could before dying himself. He was raging mad inside as he turned and walked slowly down the alleyway to his car around the corner. He would get Grimes and soon, he promised his dead partner. He would take great pleasure in putting a bullet between his eyes and watch him die.

Lou finished giving his statement to the police and told Shamus that he was going to Eddie's to unwind. He had killed men before in his job as a Chicago Policeman but this was the first time he had taken a life as a civilian. It was different this time but he would have to deal with it and move on.

He went across the street and talked to Jimmy to settle him down. "They won't bother you anymore my friend that I promise."

Lou got back in his car and sat there for a few minutes thinking about what he had just done. His partners sat there with him, silent but anxious to talk.

Wyatt finally spoke out. "You did good Lou, that polecat needed killing and he got what he had coming."

"He would not have lasted that long in Tombstone," Virgil added. "He'd be dead in the street or hanging from a tree by now. I won't be shedding any tears for him and neither should you."

Lou looked at his friends and said "I'd like to thank you guys for what you did back there. You had my back. I could be dead right now."

The ghosts began to chuckle. "Just what we need Lou another dead Earp."

Lou laughed to himself and was starting to settle down. "Let's get over to Eddie's so I can drink whiskey in front of you."

Virgil piped up "looking forward to that cousin, let's get going."

Chapter 39

Eddie's was abuzz with talk about the shooting and how Lou had helped the police gun down a couple of mad dogs. Beer and whiskey flowed freely and in no time Lou had quite a load on.

Eddie told Lou he was good for business but it was late and time for him to go home. It was only across the street but at times it seemed to take forever.

Morgan got an uneasy feeling coming out of the saloon but couldn't put his finger on it. "Something's up Lou," he said. "I can't see it but I know something's not right. Can you feel it Virgil?" he asked.

Virgil didn't get to answer because suddenly there was a black sedan screaming around the corner heading for Lou. The car would have run him over for sure if it was not for Wyatt screaming in his ear to drop and roll to the right curb.

The car missed him by inches and by that time Lou had come to his senses and had raised his pistol at the car, the driver, the tires, anything. In a second Lou had emptied his clip into the speeding sedan and sent it into a wild spin ending up next to a light pole with the windows blown out.

People came running out of Eddie's and over to Lou to see how he was while others ran to the sedan to check the driver. It was Frank Crown. He had been shot in the shoulder and had numerous cuts over his face and hands as the car windows shattered when the car was sent into a spin. He was raging like a mad dog as Eddie grabbed him and hauled him from the car and two other men from the bar dragged Crown kicking and screaming into the bar and threw him into a small storage room.

"Call the police," Lou yelled to a guy that was next to the phone and he entered the room to confront the madman who had just tried to kill him.

Frank was screaming his head off about losing his friend earlier in the day and how he had missed the man that was responsible. He tried to ram into Lou and maybe knock the gun from his hand but was only met by a pistol butt across the face. "I hate you Grimes," Frank howled. "If it's the last thing I do, I'm going to kill you and piss on your grave. The word is out on you and soon you'll be as dead as Benny."

Frank continued to ramble to himself and was out of his head mostly because of pain and frustration. "I told Benny these stupid robberies were a waste of time and bad luck and things would have been different, really different if that little shit Simms hadn't heard us talking about the museum score in the Diner and beat us to it. If he wasn't already dead, I'd kill him myself."

Lou's ears picked up everything this animal was saying and didn't push it any farther. Ten minutes later Shamus came through the storage room door, looked at Frank and over to his friend saying "didn't you get enough excitement this morning Lou?"

The police took Frank away, kicking and screaming which brought the tension levels down considerably. "Can I buy you a beer Lou?" Shamus asked.

"No my friend," he replied. "A shot of whiskey and a police escort across the street will do. It's been a hell of a day."

He didn't even look around for the Earps, just went to his room and fell asleep on his bed with his clothes on.

.

Chapter 40

Lou woke early to the sounds of someone playing cards. He cracked an eye open to confirm that he was indeed in his own room. He sat up and pulled his clothes around so that everything fit again.

The Earps were in the middle of a card game and Morgan was accusing Virgil of cheating because he was winning all the time.

Wyatt looked over at Lou and said "look brothers, our cousin is alive. Never seen a man sleep so much as you, you need to get yourself a mean old barnyard rooster and set it up on the window yonder. He'd get your sorry ass out of that thing you're calling a bed."

"It's too early for you Earps," Lou said as he rose and headed for the door.

"Where are you off to cousin? Can't you take a little ribbin this early in the morning?" Morgan asked.

"Gotta piss," Lou answered. "You should try it," Lou said, "Oh yeah," he jabbed, "you're dead."

Virgil stood up and was about to follow Lou out the door. "Where's the outhouse?" he asked, "didn't see any around."

"Down the hallway, you heathen," Lou answered. "We don't piss outside anymore."

Virgil was shocked. "You do your business in your house?" he asked, "in a little room? Don't call me no heathen."

Lou walked down the hallway trying to explain to Virgil that toilets had been invented and you could do your business and just flush it away.

They went into the bathroom and Lou showed Virgil how the toilet worked, and the sink. Lou turned on the tap and water came out of the faucet including hot water.

Virgil looked all over the place for the creek or spring that the water was coming from, but couldn't find it. But hot water, that was another story for another day. It was just too damn early.

Back in his room, Lou boiled some coffee and tried to explain how the hotplate worked and about electricity but it was just too hard so he just called it his little steel campfire. He couldn't afford a toaster so he bent up a metal clothes hangar and put it on the element. It made great toast. Yesterday he bought some strawberry jam. It was going to be a feast.

After finishing his breakfast he broke down the 9mm and cleaned it thoroughly. The Earps watched intently and were amazed at how the gun worked and the fact that it held 14 rounds hidden in the handle.

As Lou set about getting his shit together he remembered what had happened the day before and was pleased no one got hurt that didn't need to. Now that he was alone with his posse he sat on the bed again and reminded them of what he had heard the previous night from Frank Crown.

That crazy man had given them a huge piece of the puzzle they were trying to build. How did Whitie Simms get a hold of Wyatt's gun? It must have been in the museum the night he broke in and robbed the place. Question was why the gun wasn't on the list of stolen items and more so, where was all the gold and silver now?

Lou knew in his gut that Whitie had fenced it but to whom? Who in their right mind would buy anything that valuable from a lowlife like Whitie Simms?

He told his ghostly team that they were going to go back down to Barnaby's Row and continue to ask questions until something came up. Before that he wanted to see Benny again to let him know that the goons that worked him over awhile back were out of the picture and wouldn't harm him anymore.

Lou and his team of ghostly specters agreed that Whitie had fenced the valuables quietly in order to get cash to pay Donavon off but who would he go to? They walked down to the corner and up to Benny's newsstand.

"Hey Benny!" Lou yelled, before coming around to the front of the stall. "You workin or takin a nap?" Lou asked.

Benny smiled back, "g-g-good to see you Lou, g-g-glad you c-c-came b-buy."

Lou told Benny about his run-in with Frank Crown and Benny Smalls and how it all washed out. Benny thanked Lou by shaking his hand until it hurt.

The ghosts were looking at the little bruised and beaten man and told Lou that Benny needed a gun. No one deserved to be beat like that. Lou looked at the little man and nodded.

Benny was getting really excited. "Lou you're p-p-pretty hot s-s-stuff around h-h-here l-lately. Everyone is t-t-talking ab-bout how you're the n-n-new sh-sheriff."

"Thanks my friend," Lou said as he walked away. "Stay safe."

Before Lou could get ten feet away, Benny looked around the counter opening. "Hey L-Lou, come b-b-back for a m-m-minute. I g-got s-some news for you."

Lou went back and waited for Benny to come out of his shack. "There's r-rumors f-floating around the street th-that the l-loot f-from the museum heist m-m-might be surfacing. Alice down on B-Barnaby's Row got a m-m-message to me asking you to come d-d-down and s-see her."

"Thanks Benny," he said. "Shamus will probably be dropping by to see you too. Can you tell him what you just told me?" Lou asked.

Benny nodded, "s-sure th-thing sh-sheriff."

Lou and the Earps walked back to the car, Virgil looked over and said "this day's starting out all right Sheriff," and he snickered.

They drove down to Skid Row and Lou noticed that his ghostly cousins were very quiet. "What's up you guys?" he asked.

"That's a pretty tough area to walk around in," Virgil answered. "You are going to have to be sharp."

"That's why you guys are here, isn't it?" Lou smiled.

"We can tell you where they are and sometimes what they're thinking, but the rest is up to you," Wyatt came back.

The rest of the drive was just as quiet but once in the Skid Row area everyone seemed to want to talk at once. "Which way are we going Lou?" Virgil asked. "Reminds me of Tombstone, the day of the gun fight, no one in the streets, everyone just waiting to see what's going to happen."

Wyatt was looking around "Hell, you're right," he said, "been here before."

Before they started out, Lou made sure he had all his toys, both pistol and shotgun and a present. He knew where Alice liked to hang out but that was a ways from here and it was all in the open.

Virgil stayed at Lou's side and Morgan and Wyatt were about twenty paces in front, looking in doorways and alleyways.

Alice was where she always was, sitting on the step of her favorite soup kitchen trying to catch the heat of the inside every time the door opened. She saw Lou coming up the street and said to herself "he's a brave man." Too bad she didn't see the three ghosts that were protecting him.

Lou walked up to her and gave her a big smile. "We keep hanging out Alice people are going to start talking."

"I'm too much woman for you Grimes," she chuckled. "You couldn't handle the pace."

The ghosts spread out a little and kept alert as Lou sat down and pulled out his flask of whiskey from his pocket. "Nights are getting colder Alice," Lou said. "You're going to have to find some place to stay warm."

She pulled on the flask and Lou surprised her again with a heavy winter coat that had been on a coat rack at Eddie's forever "got you a little something to take the chill off."

Alice smiled warmly at Grimes and put the coat on immediately and as the warmth started to surround her for the first time in many months, she relaxed a little and looked at the man next to her. "Been causing quite a flap these days Lou. You're really pissing people off with all your questions and I hear you're shooting people."

Lou chuckled "that's what I do best Alice, always making friends." He lit up a cigarette and gave the rest of the pack to her along with the flask. "Why am I here Alice, now that the pleasantries are out of the way?"

She looked up at him from the warmth of her new coat and began. "Word around town is that the loot from the museum heist has shown up at Ruby's Pawn Shop over near Chinatown and she's bragging all over the place that she put it to Whitie Simms good. He took the stuff over there and told her that it was his grandmother's inheritance and he wanted to sell it. Ruby's telling anyone that will listen how she stiffed him good and made a killing."

"It was only a matter of time," Lou said. "People do like to talk," and with that he stood up to leave.

"Lou," Alice said grabbing his trench coat. "Donavon's men are asking around about you; you've got to be careful."

They were just as careful leaving the area as they were coming in. No sense ending the day badly.

"That's an evil place back there," Wyatt stated as they climbed back into the car. "There're a lot of varmints living back there."

Lou agreed with Wyatt but added that a few good people had to also. "Let's take a drive down by Chinatown before we call it a day," he added. "Ruby's Pawn Shop is located down there and I want to drive by a few times just to case the joint out before we go in tomorrow. Maybe park and watch the shop a bit, just to check the street."

They all agreed with this plan and after a couple of passes around the shop Lou parked half way up the block and settled in.

He looked over the paper containing the list of missing jewels, coins and artifacts. "We have to know what we are looking for when we go in there, so study this list closely."

After they looked over the list Wyatt said "we're going to go take a walk and Virgil will stay with you and Morgan and I will mosey around a little bit and get back to you."

The two ghosts moved out into the street and walked closer to Ruby's Pawn Shop. Virgil looked over at Lou and asked "do you really expect to find museum loot in there?"

Lou answered him quickly, "if she hasn't moved it by now, then yes, we stand a good chance of seeing it. Chances are she is not only bragging about it but wants to show it off a little. It will be the museum's loot alright," he said. "Whitie's grandparents are long dead and didn't have a plug nickel to call their own."

Moments later Wyatt and Morgan came back to the car. "Pretty busy place around here for looking so quiet," Morgan said. "If you weren't lookin, you'd miss all that company she's got watching the place. We counted five all toll. Two in the shop, out of sight behind the inner office door and three in the street just hanging around or watching from hideout places in the upper windows and they're all packing heat."

"That's enough for today," Lou said. "Let's get back to Eddie's and go over what we dug up today.

The guys walked into the bar and Lou sat at his regular spot and took out the lists and statements on the museum heist. There had been a fair bit of damage inside the museum but nothing that couldn't be repaired the report said. The jewels were one of a kind and the coins were rare so they would be easy to spot.

Eddie brought Lou a beer and gave him the messages that had come in that day. There were some about work, Shamus wanted him to call and there was a message from Stella reminding him that tomorrow was the last racing day of the season. He was going to have to make it or he'd never hear the end of it.

Lou and the ghosts were so busy talking about the loot, Ruby's shop and the muscle outside they missed Eddie coming up with more beer. When Eddie got closer he started to shake his head. "Lou," he said, "I'm worried about you buddy. I've been watching you for days now and you're talking to yourself more and more."

Lou looked up from what he was doing and looked at Eddie and then his invisible partners. "I know Eddie," he replied, "but it's the only way I can remember shit these days." Lou had recently realized he could communicate with the ghosts with his thoughts and made a mental note to do just that when he was around other people.

With the plan set, Lou was ready to call it a night but as they walked across the street heading for the Biltmore he told his ghostly partners that they were in for a treat tomorrow, "we're going to the horse races and we're going to make a fortune."

The last day of the season at Palisades Park was a big deal. Thousands of people would be there and Lou was going to be sure he was one of them.

Chapter 41

Lou was up early, he thought, but the Earps were already there. He dressed quickly and they walked down to Benny's, picked up a racing form and asked how he was feeling. "Much b-b-better, Lou," he replied. "Everybody k-k-keeps coming b-b-by to s-s-see how I am."

Lou told him he'd see him later and headed back to his room, trying to explain to his cousins what horse racing was all about and why so many people loved it so much.

The excitement of the race and a chance to make a lot of dough was like a drug to people like Lou but his unwanted guests figured it was like stampede day when they raced around town when a cattle drive came in and everybody bet on the winner.

Lou had to agree it sounded pretty close.

He showed them how to read the racing form and pick a horse they thought might win. He even ponied up money so they could try. For Lou it was the same old Hail Mary long shot.

His horse was called "Sunny Day," at 40 to 1, while the Earps played more conservatively and picked a horse named "Proud Mary," at four to one.

The track was just like Lou knew it was going to be. There were thousands of people having a great time visiting, drinking beer and making bets.

The Earps were truly amazed at just how many people there were. They walked up to the front gates and Lou stopped off to talk to Saul Gronski and had two hotdogs before going in. Saul gave him shit for not coming around more but Lou told him that he was looking for who killed Whitie Simms.

Saul too, had heard that Ruby's Pawn Shop was the place to be and that Donavon had been asking questions about Lou and his new job.

Before Lou went in, Saul told his friend that he'd be moving his stand uptown for the winter and could be found on West Lake Street, next to the Chicago Theatre. He expected Lou to visit, Lou agreed that he would.

In through the massive doors they went and the Earps were silent as they looked around the huge hall. Lou told the ghosts to be ready to meet one amazing woman as he strolled up to Stella's window and stood there with a sheepish grin on his face.

Stella looked up from what she was doing and for a brief second Lou thought he saw her smile. That went away quickly as she gave him the Stella face. "You're back," she said. "Haven't learned your lesson yet, have you Grimes," she scolded. "You couldn't let me have the last day of the season to be peaceful."

Lou was taken aback; he had expected a different welcoming. "Women!" he said to himself.

"Well?" Stella continued "what revelation do you have for me today Mr. Grimes?"

"I missed you too doll," Lou came back quickly. "Last day and I'm here to play," he said. "I'm going to throw you a curve today Stella," he continued. "Being it's the last day of the season and all, I'm making two bets today to double my luck."

She sat back and looked at him like it was the first time they had ever met. "Really?" she replied in shock. "Did you fall on your head or something; are you really cheapo Lou Grimes? I thought I had you figured out Lou and there you go throwing me a curve ball."

"Now she's just taunting me," he thought. "Well I'm not going to play her game," he said to himself. "Yes, Miss Jones, today is a new day and I feel lucky, so I'm going to play two races today, 'Sunny Day' in the fourth race to win." He didn't get to finish what he wanted to say when she was on him again.

"Forty to one, now that's the Lou Grimes I know," she jabbed.

"And 'Proud Mary' in the fifth."

Stella just about fell off her seat, "you're placing a bet at four to one?" she asked.

"You've got that right sister, now hand over them stubs so I can go enjoy my races.

Stella didn't know what to say. She just watched him walk away and noted "is he talking to himself?"

Lou sat in his favorite seat and gazed out onto the track. Hard to believe it was the last day of the season. "You know she really likes you, don't you Lou," Virgil finally had to say something.

"I agree Wyatt piped in. She sat right up when you came to her window."

"I didn't even have to be near her to hear her heart racing," Morgan snickered.

Lou looked at the ghosts and gave them a disgusted look. "Who, Stella?" he asked. "You guys have been dead too long. She insults me every time I come near her. She's a pain in my rump."

"He's got it too!" Morgan said to his brothers. "He just doesn't know it yet."

Lou was finished talking to these crazy spooks, he had a race to win. That didn't happen either. True to form "Sunny Day" was not so sunny for Lou and to make things even worse, "Proud Mary" won by two lengths.

As he walked up to Stella's window to collect his winnings, he could see she was astounded. "You actually won Lou?" she said, "I can't believe it."

"Me neither doll face," he replied.

He was about to leave but stopped and asked her a direct question. "What are you going to be doing for work until Spring Stella?"

Her face softened a bit and she answered quietly, "something will come up, it always does." Lou nodded at her and walked away.

"You better be throwing a rope around that gal before she gets away cousin" Wyatt commented.

Lou thought about what Wyatt had just said and took a quick a glance back to her window. She was watching him leave.

He got his head back in the game and smiled and thanked his cousins for the $20 and he was sure going to spend it right in front of them.

"Let's get going," Virgil said. "We've got a murderer to find."

They jumped in the car and drove down towards Chinatown and Ruby's Pawn Shop. Before going in they parked on the street again and looked around for a minute or two.

"Only two out there right now," Virgil said "one in the doorway, down about half a block and the other in that second story window just across the street."

"It's almost like she's expecting us, isn't it boys?" Lou replied. "Let's not disappoint her then."

Lou got out of his car and was walking up the street to Ruby's shop when he caught the glint of a rifle barrel as the sun peeked through the clouds. "You see that Wyatt?" Lou asked as they continued on.

"It's going to be an interesting morning cousin," Wyatt replied.

Lou walked through the door of Ruby's Pawn Shop and stopped just inside to look around. The Earps did not. They moved right into the shop and began looking around at everything, including the shotgun that was under the counter and the two muscle heads that were just out of sight.

The Earps continued their hunt as Ruby came out of the back room and put on a phony smile she liked to use to throw suckers off their game.

"She's got that gun pointed right at you Lou," Virgil let him know.

Unknown to Ruby, Lou had his own shotgun at the ready under his trench coat, but for now he would wait.

"How can I help you mister?" Ruby asked. Lou went into his planned speech that he and the boys had cooked up the night before. He moved closer and he could see Ruby tensing up.

He put on a stupid smile and said "looking for an anniversary present for my wife, married ten years this

Wednesday and I'm going to take her out to dinner and surprise her with a necklace or something."

Ruby relaxed a little and watched as Lou went around the shop and looked in all the display cases, asking questions about this and that.

He was picking things up as he was asking questions and actually dropped a glass pin that shattered on the dirty floor. "I'm so sorry ma'am," he said. "Hope it wasn't too expensive, only got ten bucks to spend but the little woman's worth every dime."

He continued to move around the room as did the ghosts and both came across what they were looking for at the same time; the museum robbery jewels.

"That stuff's too expensive for your blood mister," she said. "You need to be looking over to the left there," as she pointed to a cheap display case.

Lou looked at her again with the stupid smile and said that she was probably right and moved over to the other display case and made it look like he was really studying the pieces. He wasn't though, he had already found what he was looking for, the missing pieces of jewelry and coins along with a few odds and ends from the old museum had been right in front of him when he was looking in the expensive showcase display.

Lou needed to keep up his act in the shop in order not to alarm Ruby in any way. He picked out a necklace for $8.50 and brought it to the counter to pay for it. The Earps were right there next to him, trying to get his attention.

Ruby was ringing up the sale when Wyatt got Lou's attention and pointed to the display case. "That's Bunny's harmonica and pocket watch in there Lou." The other brothers agreed with Wyatt and were looking closely at the harmonica.

Lou sensed it was time to leave and call in the cavalry but first he had to get out of the shop.

Ruby finished the paperwork on the necklace and put it in a small bag handing it over to Lou. He moved toward the door and got a hold of the handle when Ruby spoke up from behind him. "Thank you for your business, I'm sure your wife will love the necklace, Mr. ?"

Lou looked back at her as he was leaving. "The name is Grimes, Lou Grimes."

It was like Ruby had stuck her finger in a light socket, the shock was so intense. Lou Grimes was in her store, snooping around. "It couldn't be good," she thought.

Lou was now outside the store but he was also out in the open. He couldn't resist sticking it to Ruby when he told her his name but now he had to get to his car and get to Shamus as fast as he could.

The Earps spread out as they retreated to the car to alert Lou to any danger and it was quick coming. Ruby ran out the door of her shop and screamed at her men in the street and they began attacking.

Lou was close to his car when the gunfire opened up. He stopped behind a utility pole just as a bullet came slamming into the wood that was shielding him from the window across the street. He lifted up his shotgun and let both barrels go at the same time, destroying the window and setting fire to the curtains.

Both men ran out of Ruby's shop at the ready only to be met by automatic gunfire and the deadly roar of Lou's shotgun.

These cowards had no stomach for this kind of firepower and fired wildly before retreating back into Ruby's shop only to be met with white hot rage from her about their lack of courage.

The gun battle, momentarily over, Lou jumped back into his car, started the engine and roared away. He was at least ten miles from Eddie's but only managed to get two miles before the engine failed and he came to a halt in the middle of the street.

Steam was hissing heavily out of the front of the engine and any water that had been in the radiator was now on the ground. Upon closer inspection, Lou found a bullet hole in the upper right corner of the radiator which meant one of the thug's rounds had gotten lucky and he was going nowhere.

He leaned against his crippled car trying to think of a way to get help. The Earps completed a quick look around and were convinced that they were indeed alone and safe for the moment.

Morgan came up to Lou and got his attention quickly. "That was Bunny's harmonica and pocket watch in that display case, along with all that loot. How the hell did Bunny's harmonica and pocket watch get into the pawn shop in Chicago in 1945?"

Chapter 42

"Are you sure they belong to Bunny?" Lou asked.

"Do you think I wouldn't remember something I took out of a man's mouth and threw down the street a hundred times because he didn't know how to play it? The damn thing was busted and he played it all the time," Wyatt said as he joined Morgan and Lou, "and that timepiece! That timepiece is stopped at 2:15 and the glass is broken inside because that's the time it stopped when I kicked Bunny in the ass for sleeping on the sidewalk. It's his Lou, it's his and what the hell is it doing here? It was in with that part of the loot from the museum robbery, so it must have come from there."

Whitie must have scooped them up that night he was filling his bag," Lou said.

Wyatt was still shaking his head. "What was Bunny's harmonica and watch doing in the Beaton Museum? Hell this is old Bunny, from Tombstone for Christ's sake."

Lou pushed the car to the side of the street and continued to walk back to Eddie's or at least the trolley line where he could get a ride there.

At the same time Ruby was in a major panic. She couldn't believe that Lou Grimes was actually in her shop and she let him get away. He had caused major damage to her organization by having one of her muscles killed and another put in jail. What was worse was that she was putting Donavon's men in danger when he had only loaned them to her while she was looking for replacements.

She was going to have to phone Donavon and try to explain what was going on and she knew he wasn't going to like it.

It took more than a half an hour for her to get her nerve up to contact the crime boss. She had to tell him that Grimes had been sniffing around her shop looking for clues about who might have killed Whitie Simms. It was also true that after getting a phone call from the track, she had sent her goons out to get her money back. According to her men Whitie was already dead by the time they got there and the money was gone.

She was sure that Grimes had spotted something from the museum loot before he left and she wanted to know what Donavon wanted her to do about it.

"Whitie came to you after the museum heist and you didn't tell me?" Donavon yelled. "He owed me a lot of dough!"

Donavon wasn't happy with this news at all and told Ruby to stay where she was and not to talk to anybody as he slammed down the receiver. He was still out the money Whitie owed him and somebody was going to pay Whitie's debt. It was bad for business to let this go unchallenged.

He sat at his desk quietly and tried to make sense out of all the mess he had just been handed. A heist he didn't know about, men being killed or jailed. He was out all that money and a shitty little private gumshoe was running around the city making him look bad.

He rose from his desk and yelled out the door for his enforcers to get into his office!

They could see that Donavon was not in a good mood, so they stood still and waited for his orders.

"Get some boys together," he said. "I've got a couple of jobs I want done." In a heartbeat they were gone.

Chapter 43

It took Lou the better part of an hour to find a trolley line and follow it before one came along and he was able to make it to Eddie's some time later.

While he traveled, his mind was racing about what had just happened. He had located the museum loot but at the same time added another question to the pile he already had and at the same time, he got shot at again.

While all these questions were buzzing around in his head, the Earps were hanging their heads out the car and looking around at everything; like a dog would do when you take him for a car ride.

Lou finally walked into Eddie's and ordered two cold ones and let them roll down his throat while he rested his feet. It had been a long day and it wasn't over yet. He needed to get his car into a repair shop so he asked Eddie to get a hold of his friend down at Fred's Service Station and have his car picked up on Downy Street, Towed back and have the radiator repaired.

"What should I tell them to look for on the radiator to be repaired Lou?" Eddie asked.

"Bullet holes," he replied.

It was getting late in the afternoon but Lou phoned the Police Station and left a message for Shamus to call Eddie's as soon as possible. An hour later the phone rang and it was Shamus. "What's up Lou?" he wanted to know.

"Listen Shamus," Lou answered quickly. "Get some policemen together and get over to Ruby's pawn shop, just outside of Chinatown. I was there a few hours ago and saw the missing loot from the museum. I swear it's there in a display case in front of her counter, and Shamus," he said, "be careful, she's got muscle outside and inside the store. Phone me when you have her in custody, I need to take a closer look at the haul. I'm looking for something that could tie in to Whitie's murder."

Lou hung up and went back to his seat to talk to his partners. "Once Shamus arrests her," he said, "we will go down to the station and recover Bunny's harmonica and timepiece."

The guys sat there for most of the evening and around 11 PM the phone rang, and it was Shamus. "Did you get the loot my friend?" Lou asked. "Is the witch in jail? When can I come down to the station and look at the haul?"

Shamus told him to slow down and listen to what he had to say. "The jewels and the coins were not there. Ruby had been robbed some hours earlier and the valuables were gone. The display case was smashed and nearly everything in it was taken. It was a good thing that we got there when we did because whoever robbed the place worked Ruby over pretty good. She's in the hospital under police protection and we have police guarding the shop front and back. I believe she knows who worked her over and took the loot, but she's not talking. She will be at the hospital for at least 48 hours according to the doctors."

"I need to see that crime scene Shamus," Lou asked. "Can I meet you there tomorrow morning early? Maybe I can help."

Shamus agreed and told Lou to meet him at the pawn shop at around 7 AM.

Lou told the Earps what had happened and about the planned meeting in the morning. They all agreed that this robbery was just too much of a coincidence and they needed to look around some more, only this time the police would be there.

It was late, very late and Lou needed to sleep. He resigned himself to the fact that the Earps came and went on their own and right now he had the room to himself. It was dark as could be and Lou was moving toward some serious sleep when suddenly the door was smashed off its hinges and two dark figures entered quickly.

It was too dark to make out any faces but that didn't matter much. From out of nowhere a fist came smashing towards his face and the lights went out. He vaguely remembered a bag being slipped over his head and two very large men lifting him from his bed and dragging him down the hall.

There was no way that the other tenants didn't know what was going on but they weren't going to step in to help.

The men bounced his limp body down the stairs and banged his head into the front door as they dragged him out into the street and threw him into the trunk of a waiting car. His head was still spinning badly as the lid was slammed down and the dark took over as the car sped away.

Lou felt his stomach turn and he was only moments away from throwing up when he heard a voice in the dark.

"We're here Lou. We will get you out of this mess." It was Wyatt.

The car turned this way and that and seemed to go on forever until it suddenly stopped and he could hear muffled voices coming toward the trunk. The lid opened up but it was still too dark to make anything out with a bag on his head.

The voice in the darkness said not to make any sudden movements or he was going to lose his teeth.

Wyatt came through his head again. "Do what they tell you and we will be your eyes and ears. You're in a warehouse on the industrial side of town, inside a walled compound. Try to settle down and we will fan out and try to find a way to get you out of here."

With that Lou knew he was alone again.

Two very large sets of hands grabbed him by his shoulders and nearly lifted him off the ground as they moved him forward. He was being moved into the building, up a set of stairs and down a long hallway. He could hear a large door being rolled back and Lou was led to the centre of a very large empty room.

His captors turned him around and sat him down on a hard wooden chair before taking the bag off his head and turning on two large bright flood lights to shine on his face.

"You've been a real pain in my ass Grimes," came a voice from behind the lights, "and you're going to answer a couple of questions before I break you into little pieces and throw your dead body into the river to feed the crabs."

Lou regained all his faculties and was checking his jaw to see if it still worked. "I'm not telling you dirt bags anything," he said, "and your monkey over there hits like a girl."

That statement got Lou another hard smash in the ear. It really hurt but Lou wasn't going to show them any fear. There was only one guy that was doing all the talking the other was silent in the background.

The Earps returned and stood around Lou while looking at his attackers. Virgil told Lou that the place was easy enough to get out of but they still hadn't found out how to overpower the two apes.

"What do you know about the museum robbery Grimes?" the voice asked, "and what's with you getting all those men killed?" The man in the dark was getting angrier because Lou wasn't answering his questions.

"You can go to hell and get your own answers, you cheap for hire punk," Lou stated.

"You're going to talk or I'm going to start breaking bones, you no talent private dick," the voice growled and moved forward on Lou to start the pain but before he could get to Lou, he fell to the floor and was out cold. The room was quiet.

"I knew something wasn't right," Morgan stated.

The other enforcer came out of the dark and stood Lou up. "Are you okay?" he asked. "Hope I didn't hurt you too bad, had to make it look good or Billy over there would have killed you the moment we got here. You weren't supposed to walk out of here alive and that's a line I can't cross," the man said.

"Who are you?" Lou wanted to know.

Wyatt looked hard at Lou's savior and answered the question for him. "He's a law dog Lou, hiding in amongst the bad guys."

"You're a Fed?" Lou asked.

"Something like that" the man said. "It would take too long to explain and you have to get out of here."

The Earps agreed with the unknown policeman and urged Lou to get moving.

"Wait!" the policeman said. "You have to shoot me!"

"What?" asked Lou.

"You have to shoot me in the leg. It has to look like we were overpowered somehow and in the scuffle I was shot and you got away. Tell Sergeant O'Hearn, Uncle Patrick said Hi and I'm okay."

"What the hell does that mean?" Lou wanted to know.

"If he wants you to know, he'll tell you," the man said.

"We have to go now Lou," the Earps pressed.

Patrick gave Lou his pistol and showed him where to shoot. "There's lots of muscle down there he pointed. It'll hurt like hell but it will look convincing enough and don't forget to tie my hands. The rest of the mob won't be long getting here once they hear the shot."

"We gotta go, we gotta go," said Morgan.

With that Lou took the gun and shot Uncle Patrick in the leg and tied his hands with a belt.

"Get out of here before they get here," he said.

Lou didn't say another word, just took off running.

Out in the courtyard Lou jumped into the black sedan that had carried him there and screamed out of the gate into the dawn before anyone arrived.

There would be no sleep for Grimes this night because it was already 6 AM. It had already been a long night and he still had one hell of a day ahead of him.

He ditched the car down in the seedier side of town and left the keys in it. He knew inside an hour someone would steal it and that would be the end of it.

He got a ride back to Eddie's from a garbage truck that was making his rounds and promised the driver a couple of beers at the bar when he could come by.

Eddie was just in the process of waking up when Lou pounded on his door and told him he needed his car. He reluctantly handed over the keys and made Lou promise not to have people shoot holes in it again. He also told him that his car would be ready that afternoon. He told Lou he looked like shit and closed the door.

Chapter 44

Lou drove down to Ruby's Pawn Shop and arrived just as Shamus was pulling up in a squad car.

Before talking to Lou, Shamus got a briefing from the policeman that was stationed there and then came over to him. "You look like hell," he said.

"I'm getting that a lot," Lou replied.

He quickly told Shamus what had happened the night before with the kidnapping and his midnight ride. He also told Shamus about almost being beat to death then saved by a guy named Uncle Patrick.

"Who the hell is Uncle Patrick?" Lou wanted to know. "He said he knows you."

Shamus smiled and told Lou he was lucky to be alive. "Ruth at the boarding house called the police right after they dragged you out of there and we've been looking for you ever since. You met a good friend of mine last night, Patrick Monahan; he's a Fed and has been under cover for a long time. The word 'Uncle' means under cover law enforcement, something to remember if you're going to stay in this game."

"I had to shoot him to get away Shamus."

"What!" Shamus said in shock.

Lou explained why and where and Shamus shook his head in disbelief. "Only Patrick would think of something like that."

They walked into Ruby's Pawn Shop and were amazed at just how much damage there was.

The Earps walked around and then came up to Lou. Virgil said "this has been staged. The damage is too confined to specific areas, it's too neat."

Lou started to really look at what he was seeing and quietly agreed with his partners. "This is a setup Shamus," he said. "They want you to think it was a robbery to cover up what they were really after, the museum loot."

They both walked over to the smashed display case and looked inside. "Like I told you Shamus," Lou said, "it's been picked clean, not a coin, not a jewel, not a clue, nothing but a rusty old pocket watch and a badly damaged old harmonica."

Everything of value was gone and they both knew who had taken it, Donavon. "We're not going to see that stuff again," Lou said, "it's long gone and Whitie's debt has been paid."

The Earps never left the display case as Shamus and Lou continued to look around at the staged mess. Finally Shamus stood straight up and stretched his back which cracked loudly.

"Nothing to see here Lou," he said. "How about you go home and get some sleep. You look like you really need it."

Lou agreed with his friend but before they left he asked Shamus if he could take the watch and harmonica with him and return it later to the museum seeing that it was on the list of stolen items.

Shamus didn't see any harm in it and agreed to let Lou take custody of the pieces to be returned to the museum at a later date.

Lou put the two items in an evidence bag and then into his pocket. He asked Shamus to meet up with him for supper at Maude's so they could go over what they had learned today. Besides, it was Friday night and Maude's special was always spaghetti and meat sauce with the biggest meatballs you ever saw.

Back at the bar Lou returned Eddie's car and was told that his ride would be ready at the end of the day.

Over at the Biltmore, Lou found that Ruth had gotten the hinges put back on his door. He thanked her and gave her $20 for the damage and the trouble.

Back in his room, though he needed to sleep badly, he first had to confirm what he was looking at. The harmonica was indeed bent and broken and Wyatt showed Lou the damage he created to the piece when it bounced off a piece of iron as he threw it down the street.

The watch was the full confirmation though. When Lou opened it, it was indeed stopped at 2:15 and the glass crystal was broken. He needed sleep now more than ever. He asked the guys to stick around so he knew he would be safe and was asleep immediately.

The Earps sat around the table looking at the watch and harmonica. "How the hell did they get here," Wyatt wanted to know.

"He must have had them on him the day I said goodbye to him at the stagecoach," Virgil added, "and I never knew what his real name was."

It was not a coincidence that Wyatt's gun and these things were here at the same time. "We are going to have to find out why," Virgil said, "can't have a question like that hanging over us forever."

They sat around telling each other funny stories about Bunny and all the shit he used to get himself into. Virgil laughed when he told the story of the day he threw Bunny into a horse trough and told him to wash because the General smelled better than he did.

In the end they all agreed that Bunny always seemed to be in the wrong place at the wrong time. That was just who he was.

Lou woke about three in the afternoon, got dressed and had coffee. He was ready for the rest of the day and was eager to get right to it.

"We have to get down to Fred's and pick up my car before anything can happen," Lou said, "so let's get going.

He got on the next available trolley that was heading downtown and the same thing happened as before. It was a good thing no one could see what the Earps looked like with their heads hanging out the open windows.

At Fred's garage, he tossed Lou two bullets. "What's this for?" Lou asked.

"One was in the radiator but the other we found in the back of your seat. You're luckier than you think."

On the way back to Eddie's, Lou made sure the ghosts were looking for anything out of the ordinary and watching for cars that might be following. Donavon was not through with him yet, not by a long shot. From now on his guard would have to be up.

He got back to Eddie's and ordered a beer. He checked his lists one more time to confirm that the two items were from the museum. Now he had to find out how they got there and why.

He asked the Earps about what they knew about the odd little man. When did he come to Tombstone, what were his habits and did he have any friends? The Earps had to confess that they really hadn't known Bunny at all. He was just always there and had been there before they arrived in Tombstone. They understood that he had been mining for many years and he had left on the stage to Tucson soon after striking it rich.

Virgil had talked to him the day he left and Bunny had told him that he was very sick and had to see a doctor there. That was the last any of the Earps saw of him.

Finally, Lou had to ask the big question. "What was Bunny's real name?"

They all looked at each other and had to agree, they just didn't know. The odd little man that struck it rich and left Tombstone was just "old Bunny." They all agreed that Bunny was a mystery and his whereabouts after leaving Tombstone and going to Tucson needed to be investigated.

Lou would start at the library and then the state building of records of gold and silver mines owned around Tombstone in 1881.

When he got to Maude's, Shamus was waiting for him, dinner was amazing and over pie and coffee they talked about what had been happening and what needed to be done.

Shamus told Lou that Ruby was out of the hospital and wasn't saying anything about her attackers or her missing property. Lou had to agree with Ruby this time. For her to start ratting out Donavon's men to the police would mean her certain death.

Lou and the Earps were going to look deeper into why Whitie took the watch and the harmonica and at the same time he wanted Shamus to get to the City Records Department and pull up the records on the old museum so they could see who owned it before becoming the property of Chicago, maybe it would give them a clue.

Once they parted ways, Lou returned to Eddie's and sat back on his stool, trying to make sense of it all. There were so many questions and so few answers.

He was talking to his partners about what was going to happen the next day when Eddie came over and told Lou to go home. He was scaring the customers by talking to himself the way he did.

They walked out of the bar and across the street, and agreed that the City library was a good start but Shamus had to come through with the City records if this was to go any farther.

Chapter 45

Lou and his cousins were at the library early the next day trying to find anything about the museum they could but came up short. There was nothing.

They next went to the Chicago Tribune Newspaper Building and looked through the archives for anything that may have been written about the museum. That's where they got lucky. They found a small piece written about the museum being renamed from the Jessop Gallery of Antiquities to the Jim Beaton Memorial Museum. There was a picture of a middle aged woman holding an Indian headdress. They identified her as the new owner. Her name was Victoria Beaton.

While Lou was looking at the article, his cousins were reading about Al Capone and the St. Valentine's Day Massacre and were amazed at just how bad this murderer was. "He wouldn't last long in Tombstone," Wyatt said. "He would be swinging from the end of a long rope long ago."

With the information they gathered in hand, Lou and his band of would-be detectives stepped out of the building into the Chicago morning sunshine, right into a trap. They had no time to react and were immediately surrounded by two black sedans and a large Rolls Royce. They had Lou's car completely surrounded with no way to escape. Strangely no one was moving from their cars or shooting from the windows.

The Earps fanned out to try and find a way out and understand what Lou was up against. Lou stood perfectly still. Virgil was the first back. "There are six of them Lou and they're carrying a lot of guns."

Morgan appeared next to Lou and then walked up to the Rolls. "This one here has got Terry Donavon in the back seat, isn't that a special surprise."

"Keep your eyes on his muscle guys I need to know who is going to move first so I have time to put a hole in Donavon's head."

The Earps disappeared into the black sedans to watch what was going to happen. Lou still hadn't moved.

It was probably only a minute but to him it felt like forever.

"Donavon is moving towards his door Lou," Wyatt said.

Lou touched the shotgun under his trench coat. If it was going to go down, Donavon was going first he thought to himself.

The window of the Rolls slowly rolled down and from the dark interior Donavon spoke out. "We need to talk Grimes," he said. "Are you armed?"

Lou answered quickly "it pays to carry a little insurance these days Donavon. What do you want and make it fast. I gotta be somewhere."

"What say we call a truce for ten minutes Grimes and take a walk down the street?"

"I can do that," Lou said. "It's a nice sunny day and a walk will do us both good but remember *Terry* anything goes sideways during our little stroll, you'll be the first to die."

"Fair enough," Donavon said. "I'm going to step out of the car now, nice and easy and I won't be carrying a gun."

The door to the car opened slowly and out stepped a very well-dressed man. Lou was sure that what he was wearing was worth more than what Lou made in a year. He was about 6 feet, in his early 50's, clean shaven, grey temples. He carried a very expensive walking stick with a solid silver handle. It added to his commanding presence but was probably not needed to aid him in walking.

Donavon stood up straight and stretched a little coming out of the car. "Nice day for a walk Grimes, don't you think, stretch the legs, get some sun and breathe in some clean air."

Donavon started to move slowly down the street and Lou kept pace with him. He noticed the Rolls Royce was keeping pace with them too which meant that Donavon's goons were never far away.

Donavon started the conversation up first. "I think you and I got off on the wrong foot Grimes, you keep killing off my men or have them thrown in jail for no reason at all. That's not very friendly and it's bad for business."

Lou continued to keep pace with the mob boss and was waiting for his cousins to tell him when things were going to get ugly. It didn't happen.

It was Lou's turn to talk and he didn't waste a second. "You've got to train your dogs to stay in their own back yard *Terry*. They've been sniffing around my neighborhood and beating people up, including old women, just for a few bucks and other times just for the fun of it. Seeing as we are on the subject, Lou stopped and looked at Donavon, you didn't have to have Whitie killed at the track for that money. You could have waited and taken it away from him. I think killing is bad for business too *Terry*. It puts you in the spotlight."

It was Donavon's time to stop and look over at Lou. "You think I killed Whitie Simms?" he said. "You're barking up the wrong tree Sheriff. I admit that killing the little shit would have made me feel better but then who was going to pay his debt. That would be bad for business."

This news floored Grimes but he didn't show it to Donavon. "If you didn't kill the little weasel, who did?" Lou probed.

"My guys were there," Donavon stated, "but the little shit was already dead and a crowd had gathered around him. They didn't see any money."

Lou could sense Donavon was telling the truth but that didn't answer the question. Who killed Whitie Simms and where was all that money.

Donavon stopped walking and Lou knew this little meeting was over. "I'll back off if you do Grimes," Donavon said.

Lou looked over at the mob boss and replied "Chicago is a big place *Terry*; you've got plenty of space to run around in, the south side is a nice place and I live here. I intend to keep it that way."

Both men had said their peace and the conversation was over but as Donavon climbed back into his car Lou came over to the window and looked in. "*Terry*," he said, "you still owe me a new hat."

Donavon looked back at Lou and said "the name is Donavon, only my mother calls me Terry." With that, the window rolled up and the car moved away with nothing more said.

"Interesting morning," Morgan said as he appeared next to Lou in the car.

"Did you hear what he said?" Virgil continued. "His men didn't kill Whitie."

Lou was deep in thought and didn't answer right away. "All those people there and nobody saw anything. Somebody killed Whitie and right in plain sight. We have to get over to Maude's, Shamus is going to meet me there with any documents he found about the museum and I want to tell him about the newspaper article."

Shamus was again waiting for Lou as he entered the Diner and waved him over to sit down. "I was just about to order a coffee and a piece of pie, but seeing as you're here now we can get to it and have lunch later."

Lou started out by telling Shamus about the newspaper article he found at the Chicago Tribune and told him about his meeting with Donavon.

"You're lucky to be alive," Shamus said and Lou agreed.

The policeman sat back and rubbed his face with both hands. "If he didn't kill Whitie, then we're back to square one."

"What did you find at City Records Shamus," Lou wanted to know.

The policeman leaned forward and said "quite a bit actually but it's a sad tale of a lonely woman ending badly. Before the City took over the old museum it was owned by one Victoria Beaton who had inherited it from Edwin Moses years before. The place was a well known Western Antiquities Gallery back then and had quite a collection of Western Americana from around the country. Things were going well for Miss Beaton until the stock market crash in 1929 and the economy ground to a full halt. The gallery managed to stay afloat for a couple of years because of Victoria's vast fortune but eventually that faded away along with her customers and the Gallery declared bankruptcy and closed its doors. Because of her advanced age, failing health and lack of money to support herself, Victoria Beaton passed away in an old boarding house just off Barnaby's Row and was buried in a pauper's grave some place known only to the City.

"I'll keep digging," Shamus said, "but I think we're looking in the wrong direction and need to rethink the mystery. Meanwhile, the museum is still closed. I think you should get those two pieces back there so they can be removed from the list as being recovered."

Lou agreed and told Shamus that he would return them in the morning first thing.

Back at Eddie's bar Lou sat on his stool and went over his day; the library, his meeting with Donavon and the meeting with Shamus. It all seemed to be leading him to a dead end.

He was missing something; he just didn't know what it could be. He checked his messages and found a few from Abraham Schwarz. That meant he still had a job. Even though the Whitie Simms murder was taking up all his time he would have to check in with Abe in the next day or two.

Another message was a dinner invitation from Max Taylor and his wife, seeing as he missed the last one and one from Stella. It simply read "Coffee?"

Morgan had been reading over his shoulder and stepped back to chuckle. "I told you cousin," he said. "She's got her eye on you."

Lou called Morgan an asshole and told him he didn't know what he was talking about. He would call Stella later and set something up.

With that he called it a night and went to the Biltmore.

Chapter 46

The next morning Lou planned to return the watch and harmonica to the museum although the Earps complained loudly. According to the brothers, they owned the two items just as much as the museum did, maybe more.

Lou had never heard so much whining from three supposed tough guys in his life. It was finally settled, the items were going back today.

He drove to the museum and parked in front. The policeman guarding the building knew he would be coming and let him in without a challenge.

The place looked old and gloomy inside and had a hollow feeling to it. The life had been sucked out of it by years of neglect and now it was just quiet and empty.

"Creepy in here," Virgil said as he moved around the floor.

"You've got that right," Lou offered.

Grimes slowly walked up to the display cabinet that the Earps found right away. "This is it," Wyatt said. Morgan nodded his head in agreement.

"How do you know this is the one?" Lou wanted to know.

"Look here," Wyatt said pointing to some of the other things that were in the display. "This here is Bunny's old hat, that there is his rusty old gun that kept jamming whenever he tried to shoot a coyote that was coming around his camp. This here is his moth eaten old bed roll that was stamped 'US Cavalry,' he traded a drink of whiskey for it from an old Indian Dog Soldier that drifted through town. It's his stuff alright."

"How in the hell did it get here?" Wyatt wanted to know.

"I don't know," Lou offered "but the watch and harmonica was Bunny's and they belong here with the rest of his stuff. It's only right."

Lou put the two pieces into the display case and stepped back to look at them. "They belong there," he said. "So many pieces of history," he added as he looked over the rest of the display. There were belt buckles, old cowboy boots, branding irons and bibles and journals from people long dead that had a story they wanted to tell.

The bible was well-worn and according to the label had been the property of a woman named Jane Wolsley, most likely a pioneer woman from the old west and there were two journals next to it. They were equally worn and were owned by a woman named "Victoria Strong" who likely had long since passed.

"Let's get out of here Lou," Morgan said. "This place is really depressing."

They left the museum knowing that Bunny's things would be well cared for when the museum opened up again. They then drove back to Eddie's bar to talk about their next moves.

The Earps had all kinds of ideas to try, all of which Lou dismissed as crap for one reason or another. The phone rang as Lou was having an internal argument with Virgil about grabbing one of Donavon's men and seeing if he knew anything about Whitie's killer.

Lou wasn't ready to start a new war with the mob boss just yet and told Virgil he was an idiot.

Eddie called Lou to the phone and told him Stella was on the line. Lou took the receiver and told the cousins to go sit down.

He said hello and the first thing out of her mouth was "you were suppose to call me you big lug."

Lou said he was sorry but the Whitie thing was really eating up all his time. "That's no excuse Grimes," she came back. "I needed to talk to you about Whitie's funeral."

"What funeral?" he asked. "I didn't know there was going to be one."

"Me neither," Stella said, "and that's the strange thing Lou, nobody does. I tried to phone Edith and offer her my condolences but she's not answering. I'm getting concerned Lou," she said.

Lou agreed that it was a little strange and he would give Shamus a call and see if he had heard anything. Stella told him to get back to her as soon as he heard anything and gave him her phone number.

Lou phoned Shamus at the station and asked him to check the morgue to see if Whitie's body had been released to anyone. A cold beer later Shamus called back with the news that Whitie's body was still there and the coroner was beginning to make inquiries about its removal.

Grimes told Shamus that Stella had phoned and asked about any service that would be taking place but she was unable to get in touch with Whitie's mother.

"Maybe she just doesn't want to talk to anyone just yet." Shamus said that he would look into it and Lou called it a night.

The next morning Lou was banging on Stella's door after talking to her the night before and coffee was the order of the day and maybe some toast and jam.

Stella had never been to Maude's before and was quite pleased with the place and Maude too.

"You finally bring a girl around," Maude said, "it's about time."

Lou brushed her off and ordered coffee and toast before sitting down in his booth.

Grimes told Stella that he had talked to Shamus the previous night and he said that he would get back to him but he wasn't waiting. "We're going over to Whitie's mother's apartment right after coffee."

Lou was finding that he was enjoying talking to Stella and gave the Earps a stern look of annoyance when they appeared and sat next to her. "Told you cousin," Morgan said, "your single days are numbered," and they all chuckled.

Light conversation about Lou's new career and what Stella was up to now lead them to speculation as to why Edith wasn't answering her phone. More questions than answers motivated them to quickly finish and drive to Edith's apartment.

They pulled up in front of the building and parked and a police car pulled in behind them and out popped Shamus shaking his head and looking at Lou and Stella.

"I should have known you wouldn't wait for my call. What were you going to do?" Shamus asked "break in? At least I got a warrant," he said, waving the piece of paper in the air. Let's check this out. There has to be a reasonable explanation."

Up the stairs they went and stopped in front of Edith's door. Shamus knocked, then knocked again and got no answer. Then he pounded on the door and called out that he was the police and wanted Edith to open the door. There was still no answer.

"You've got a warrant for Christ's sake, break it in!"

Shamus didn't have to be told again. He pushed his heavy body against the door and the door swung open. A stale smell greeted their noses.

Shamus went in first with his hand on his pistol. The Earps moved past everyone without waiting and were all over the apartment in seconds. "The place is empty Lou," Virgil said. "There hasn't been anyone here for awhile."

Lou relaxed but Shamus was still alert. They moved through the apartment to find Whitie's bed not made and neither was Edith's. Moving to the kitchen Stella called the two men over to the fridge. "Look here," she said, "the milk is sour and there's a half loaf of stale bread on the counter."

Everyone looked at the table at the same time and saw a teacup that was half full and drying. There was a piece of toast lying half eaten on a saucer. "Something is terribly wrong," Shamus said. They would have to leave now because this was now a crime scene and he was going to call the station house.

As they left the apartment Stella noticed that Edith's coat and hat were missing along with her shoes and purse. "No self respecting lady would leave the house without her purse," she said going out the door.

The police went over the apartment from top to bottom and found nothing. They canvassed the neighbors and got nowhere either. No one had seen Edith for days.

Lou and Stella headed back to Eddie's for a beer and then back over to Maude's for dinner. They talked most of the evening about Edith's disappearance, her apartment and how eerie it looked with the teacup and old toast.

Lou asked Stella about how she was doing, looking for work now that the track had closed for the season. She answered immediately, "I'm a survivor Lou you know that. I've got two other roommates to keep my share of the rent low and have picked up work here and there to keep food on the table and lipstick in my purse. I did a short stint over at the Tribune running copy to and from the editor but he wanted me to deliver more than the news, so I punched him in the face and left. For now I'm working part time in an insurance company, typing up claim reports."

Lou told her that he'd keep his eyes and ears open to any other opportunities and Stella thanked him. "Anything that keeps the bear from scratching at my door," she said.

Lou took her back to her apartment and promised to keep her "in the know," if anything came up about Edith. She thanked him for dinner and promised to do the same.

He walked back out to his car and the air around him exploded with laughter, and questions "Why didn't you kiss her you big lug?" Wyatt wanted to know.

"You didn't even hold her hand," Morgan said as he climbed into the car.

"She was shaking the whole time you were with her," Virgil laughed.

"You should have kissed her. I'm pretty sure she wouldn't have slapped you," Wyatt added as he came back to the car and burst out in laughter.

The drive back was just one dig after another but Lou wasn't listening. He was sorting things out in his head. Trying to find that one thing that he was missing.

Chapter 47

Lou woke the next morning to his unwelcome "guests" talking loudly in his room about what they had seen or not seen the day before at the museum and also what they saw at Edith's apartment.

The more they argued amongst themselves the more Lou wanted them to go away. It was too early for children to be fighting.

That old saying that bad things make good newspaper copy never rang more true today.

Lou walked down to Benny's newsstand for his morning paper and there on the front page was a picture of Edith Simms with a caption across the front page in big black letters "MISSING MOTHER – HAS THE PALISADES PARK MURDERER STRUCK AGAIN?"

Some asshole reporter had been tipped off about Edith's disappearance, tied Whitie's death to it and was saying that the police should be looking for her body.

"I hate reporters," he said to himself as he walked back to Eddie's for a coffee and breakfast of champions, a beer.

He knew this was going to get around quickly and would bring out all the nut jobs to speculate and look for ways to make money off of it.

Shamus walked into the bar around noon and found Lou still looking over the paper, trying to figure out how the slimy reporter got hold of the information and turned it around so badly.

Shamus told him that there were cops in the department that tipped off reporters about stories for money and they were good at keeping their heads down.

He brought Lou up to speed on Edith's disappearance and told him that they were treating the case as suspicious for now. There were no clues.

Lou was shaking his head as Shamus produced a piece of paper from his coat pocket and put it in front of him on the bar.

"You're gonna like this my friend," he said.

Lou looked up from the newspaper, took the folded paper and opened it. His eyes widened. In his hand was Victoria Beaton's Death Certificate.

Lou sat straight up, looking at the piece of paper in his hand.

"Where did you find this Shamus?" he said, reading the document as he was asking questions.

Shamus told him that City Records was in a mess after the Great Depression. He found the document in the old records section of City Hall that had been closed off for years.

It seemed that when Victoria Beaton's health was failing and she knew that she would not survive she gave a friend of hers, a lady that used to frequent the gallery when it was doing well, her private papers for safe keeping. If anything happened to her, the friend was to turn the documents over to the police.

"That's where we found them, tucked away in a back filing cabinet in an old part of a room."

Lou couldn't read the certificate fast enough. It was indeed a certificate of death. It read:

"Date of Death: March 3, 1931

"Place of Death: Chicago, Illinois

"Full name: Victoria Wilhelmina Beaton

"Sex: Female

"Color of Race: White

"Marital Status: Single

"Date of Birth: August 10, 1855

"Occupation: Business Owner

"Business: Art Gallery

"Place of Birth: Deadwood, South Dakota

"Name of Father: Jim Beaton

"Birth Place of Father: Florence, Arizona

"Maiden Name of Mother: Strong

"Mother's Place of Birth: Tombstone Arizona"

Lou put the document down and stared off into space.

"That doesn't make any sense Shamus," he said. "Says here that her mother never married and her name was Strong."

Shamus picked up the certificate and looked at it closer. "She took her father's name way back when for a reason we'll never know and legally changed it when she got to Chicago."

"Why would she take her father's name?" Lou asked.

"That's something we may never know my friend," Shamus added. "Deadwood was a pretty wild place back then," he offered. "Must have been pretty hard on a single mom raising a daughter in Deadwood," he added.

"How did Victoria end up in Chicago and why?" Lou asked. "Something's missing," he added, "and I can't put my finger on it, but I will."

Shamus stood up, getting ready to go when he added "that's all the documents we found Lou, not even a Bible. You know how they used to keep notes and papers in Bibles back then, but there wasn't one with her papers."

A light came on in the back of Grimes' mind. "Not a bible, Shamus my friend, a journal, Victoria Strong's journals! I need to get back to the museum fast Shamus, can you clear it with security? I need to confirm something and remove it from the museum for a while if it's okay with you?"

Shamus told Lou he didn't have a problem with it and would let security know he was on his way.

Lou got into his car and drove over to the Beaton Museum as fast as he could. The Earps were with him and were all asking questions at the same time.

"Where are we going in such a hurry Lou?" Wyatt asked.

Morgan leaned over and told Wyatt he had heard him say he was going back to the museum.

"What did you remember Lou?" Virgil wanted to know.

Grimes told them all to shut up so he could think and if his hunch was right they were all going to get some answers shortly.

He stopped in front of the building and again got by the guard easily. He went through the door and went right back to the display case containing Bunny's harmonica.

"Why are we back here cousin?" Virgil asked.

"Looks the same to me," Wyatt said.

"That's the problem" Lou stated "everything looks the same." With that he reached into the display case and removed Victoria Strong's journals.

He opened one briefly to confirm his suspicions then closed it again and confronted his ghostly partners.

"These were Victoria Strong's journals alright, but they were also Victoria Beaton's journals. She changed her name."

"Why did she do that," asked Morgan.

"I'm hoping to find the answer to that question and a few more," said Lou as he drove back to Eddie's for a nightcap and then off to his room for some light reading.

The Earps were all over Lou as he sipped his beer quietly contemplating what he might find amongst the old pages of Victoria's journals.

Chapter 48

Back in his room Grimes sat at the little table and opened Victoria's first journal.

"She was Millie Strong's daughter, says so right here in the first entry." Lou read the first entry to his excited cousins.

"Victoria Strong's Journal

"Date: July 15, 1867

"My mother, Millie Strong gave me these journals as we stood on the train platform in Deadwood holding each other's hands, before the train was to leave. She told me to take a moment each day if possible and write down my thoughts and experiences.

"I'm excited and scared all at the same time. I have never been without my mother by my side and now I am here, off to Chicago, Illinois to attend a strange new school that I have never heard of with a governess named Prudence that I only met three days ago.

"There was another parting surprise. Mother has told me that my father is alive. His name is Jim Beaton. She said that he is a miner and lives in Tombstone. I am to contact him if anything should happen to her."

"That's why she was here in Chicago. Her mother sent her away," Morgan stated.

Lou read on a little more about the scared little girl and her thoughts long ago.

"I watched her waving from the platform as the train pulled out, until I couldn't see her anymore. This is truly the saddest day of my life.

"Date: July 18, 1867

"I've never been on a train before. It's noisy and smelly. Prudence is quietly reading her book, but I can't stop looking out the window.

"Date: August 15, 1867

"I have been on this train forever. I have read all my books and Prudence is now teaching me how to crochet. Will this journey ever end?

"Date: August 20, 1867

"Prudence has allowed me to walk up and down the train car aisle which has given me the chance to stretch my limbs and study the other passengers more closely.

"I saw a real soldier today. He smiled and tipped his hat at me and there was a real Indian too.

"Date: August 29, 1867

"Finally Prudence has told me that tomorrow we will be arriving in Chicago. I make this promise to myself. I promise never to ride on a train again! It's so boring!"

The Earps were mesmerized as they listened to Lou unravel Victoria's secrets.

"Date: August 30, 1867

"As I watch the city of Chicago fill my window space with buildings upon buildings and a noise level that increases as we get closer, I take a moment to think of my mother alone in a little town called 'Deadwood' in the middle of nowhere. I miss her deeply.

"Date: September 4, 1867

"Prudence left me yesterday. She has gone off to do what governesses do and has left me in the care of my new school's Head Mistress. She seems to be a very nice lady and I'm sure we will get along.

"There are quite a few girls here and I hope to get along with all of them."

There were many entries in the journals spanning the years that Victoria grew up in Chicago and she made entries often.

Lou read on for a few hours and then told the boys he was going to bed. It had been a long day and there was still a lot to go through.

Chapter 49

Over breakfast the next day Lou continued reading Victoria's entries until he came upon something very interesting and disturbing.

"Date: May 14, 1882

"I have received a letter yesterday from mother. We have written often over the years, so many letters I have lost count, but I have them and cherish them.

"This one was different. She is gravely ill and wishes me to come home as quickly as possible. I am terribly worried about her and will leave as soon as I tell my employers of my intention and will purchase a ticket to Deadwood immediately."

"She went back to Deadwood?" Wyatt asked.

Lou just nodded.

"Date: June 12, 1882

"The train is taking forever. I hope for the best and fear the worst.

"Date: June 16, 1882

"I am heartbroken. I am too late. Mother has passed away from pneumonia some weeks back and I am only just getting here.

"Belle has been with me all the time. She has been my mother's best friend and partner and I'm here now and we talk about her every day.

"I have spent much of my time at the gravesite, trying to feel closer to her after all this time. I feel a great emptiness inside me that will probably never go away."

"Tough break," Morgan said.

Lou read on.

"Date: June 23, 1882

"Belle called me to her office today and showed me my mother's Last Will and Testament. All that was hers is now mine: clothes, jewelry and a vast sum of money she had made over the years along with the sale of her half of 'The Purple Door' to Belle.

"It means nothing without her."

"Wait a minute," Wyatt said. "'The Purple Door?' wasn't that a famous whorehouse in Deadwood?"

"Imagine that," Morgan said. "Victoria's mother owned 'The Purple Door.' Bin there a couple of times myself over the years."

Lou continued reading and was now keenly interested in Victoria's journey.

"Date: June 24, 1882

"Before leaving Belle's office yesterday she gave me a sack of correspondence, and leaflets that the post office had brought over to her when mother passed away.

"I took the sack from Belle and told her that I would be finalizing mother's estate and going back to Chicago in a couple of days.

"Date: June 25, 1882

"I sit at the gravesite for the last time and I promised myself that I would open the small sack of letters and read them to her this last time.

"To my horror there was a telegram amongst the letters from my father to my mother. It read that he was sorry that he had not followed her to Deadwood many years ago and was also sorry that he had not ever met their daughter, Victoria.

"It said that he was in Tucson, very ill and wanted to see her one last time. Will my heart ever stop aching? I must go to him at once and tell him about mother's passing.

"Date: June 30, 1882

"I didn't believe that I could dislike anything more than the train, but I was wrong.

"The stagecoach wins. For three days and two nights I have endured dust, bad roads, no roads at all, the smell of sweaty horses and worse still the smell of sweaty people. I have no idea why people would want to live out here.

"Date: July 1, 1882

"I met the Marshall soon after I arrived in Tucson and enquired about my father, Jim Beaton. I was told to talk to a lady at a boarding house because she knew where I could find him.

"It was yet another sad day in my life. Will this pain never end? My father, a man I had never known has passed away of lung consumption some time back.

"He lived in the boarding house up until he died and the kind lady, Emmy Hemsley, had been with him at the end.

"I can't believe I have lost both parents in such a short span of time. I truly am alone."

"Never knew a person could write so much," Wyatt said.

"We are very lucky she did," Lou replied. "I have a feeling she's going to be able to answer a lot of questions for us."

"Date: July 8, 1882

"I spent a lot of time at the gravesite telling my father about his true love and how strong a woman she had been. I have taken a broach from mother's belongings and buried it in his grave, next to the headstone so that he would always have something of hers close by.

"His marker reads:

"Jim 'Bunny' Beaton 1817 to 1882"

"I will remember those words."

Wyatt damn near jumped out of his ghostly skin and Morgan started to choke.

"Bunny?" they all said it at once.

"It's Bunny? Bunny is Victoria Beaton's father? Damn when did that happen?" asked Virgil.

"Jim and Millie must have been together before we arrived in Tombstone," Morgan said.

"I'm going to stop reading for now. We've got enough to think about for one day." Lou said.

The brothers faded away and Lou could still hear them talking.

"Bunny Beaton, who the hell would have seen that coming?"

Chapter 50

The next day was to have been devoted to reading Victoria's entries but that was not to be. A body had been found in the river, an aged female body. It had been discovered in amongst the rocks downriver about three miles.

It was in bad shape. Between the water, the pounding of the rocks and the crabs, it was hard to make identification. It didn't matter. To the press it was Edith Simms and they went crazy with it.

Lou went with Shamus to the morgue to try to make an I.D. but it was impossible. She would be a Jane Doe until proven differently.

The lead headlines in the morning papers read "MYSTERY WOMAN FOUND IN RIVER – POSSIBLY EDITH SIMMS – FOUL PLAY SUSPECTED!"

For the next two days and nights Lou, the Earps and Shamus followed any clue or lead they were given but to no avail. The question remained. "Was this woman Edith Simms?"

"This trail is cold Lou," Wyatt said "time to move on down the trail partner and let the police do what they have to do."

Lou had to agree.

Once again the guys found themselves at Maude's because it was quieter there and they would be able to concentrate on Victoria's journey.

The Earps were still buzzing around the fact that Bunny was Victoria's father and couldn't wait to hear more. To anyone else looking in Lou's direction he was just a man reading a book.

"Date: July 9, 1882

"Tomorrow I will be going to the bank and the Town Hall to settle father's affairs and soon after that I will be going back to Deadwood and on to Chicago. That will be my home."

"Date: July 10, 1882

"The bank manager was very happy to see me and told me how father had completed a large business transaction with him and a large amount of money was involved. It would seem that father's Last Will and Testament left everything to mother and upon her passing, to me.

"The sum of money was staggering and I had the manager wire the fortune to my bank in Chicago."

"Wonder how much it was?" Virgil asked.

"We may never know," Lou said, "but most likely it had been a fortune in silver."

"Date: July 12, 1882

"I visited the grave one last time today and said goodbye to a man I never knew.

"The lady at the boarding house has given me father's belongings which were meager at best: an old hat, rags he used to wear, a pair of wire-rimmed glasses, a broken watch, a harmonica, a six gun and holster, bedroll and another gun with a long scrolled barrel and a dark handled grip.

"I looked at what was in front of me. It wasn't very much for a lifetime of hard work but I will cherish them forever."

Wyatt came alive, "my gun! That's my gun!" He was standing up in the Diner, pacing up and down with his voice raised and arms flailing but no one could see it but Lou. "The little bastard stole my gun Lou."

"You don't know that Wyatt," Lou said. "The last time you saw that gun was during the gunfight at the O.K. Corral and it was shot out of your hand. Bunny was probably nearby during all the dust and commotion and after you boys went back to the saloon he most likely found the gun in the dirt, put it in his saddlebag and left town, not wanting anything to do with what had just happened."

"The last time I saw Bunny was the day he left town on the stage," Virgil said. "I shook his hand and wished him well. He probably had your gun in his travel bag when I was saying goodbye."

"Well I'll be damned!" Wyatt said. "Jim 'Bunny' Beaton was just one surprise after another."

"Date: July 14, 1882

"I left Tucson today and did not look back, numb from the experience.

"Date: July 18, 1882

"I spent one night in Deadwood on my way back home. It was still a very sad time for me but I have told mother of Jim Beaton's passing and said goodbye one more time.

"I buried Jim's wired-rimmed glasses near her headstone.

"I am sure that they will be forever grateful but I've done all I can and it's time for me to leave."

"She's got my gun!" Wyatt screamed, standing right next to Lou.

Chapter 51

Date: July 25, 1882

"The train ride back to Chicago is just as hard for me as the one going to Deadwood. Strange people get on, strange people get off. There are miners, cowboys, families going who knows where and many more Indians and dust."

Date: July 26, 1882

"I read a lot and my journal keeps me busy and lets the miles roll by. I have written about everything that has happened. I think I have matured greatly during this sad adventure across the wilds of America but I yearn for it to be over and behind me."

Date: July 28, 1882

"With all that's been going on in the train, stopping and starting even a man with a goat, one thing has been the same. I have been watching a strange little man going about his business collecting things when the train stops for water or coal. He even got hold of a four foot high wooden Indian and has it in the seat next to him. His activity has been a source of amusement for me for many days.

"Date: July 29, 1882

"I met the strange little man today. His name is Edwin Moses. I was going to admonish him for being so forward but he was genuinely interested in what I was reading and I wanted to find out about the wooden Indian. I introduced myself to him as Victoria Beaton. I have decided to use my father's name from now on.

"I have found out that Edwin is a Western Antiquities Collector and has a small gallery on the south side of Chicago named after his late wife."

"That's when she changed her name!" Morgan said.

"Read on Lou," Virgil said, "sounds like she's having quite an adventure."

"Date: September 30, 1882

"I have become great friends with Edwin Moses. His interests are my interests I have discovered and I have offered to invest in his gallery for a small percentage.

"Date: October 2, 1882

"Today, to my great surprise Edwin has offered me a partnership in the gallery. It has become known as a professional establishment and rare antiquities can be displayed there and offered for sale. It was the best decision I have ever made.

"Date: February 1, 1884

"I have finally decided to display my father's artifacts along with the many others Edwin had gathered. I am proud to see them there and he was too. But not the Colt, no one knows of its existence. This piece is special to me and I will be putting it away secretly in the false bottom of a drawer in my desk. Only I will know it's there. It's a comfort to know my father is near."

Wyatt was hanging on every word. "The desk, the desk in the museum, that's where it's been all these years! I can't believe it. It would probably still be there today if that little weasel Whitie Simms hadn't discovered it while rooting around the desk looking for valuables. That gun has had quite the journey!"

"Date: April 11, 1902

"Another sad day has come for me, Edwin my dear friend and business partner passed away today. He had been ill for some time; nevertheless it was still a great shock.

"Date: April 18, 1902

"I just came back from the Lawyers today. Edwin has signed everything over to me. I now own the Jessop Gallery.

"Date: July 5, 1904

"The Gallery is a success and business is booming. People are practically storming the building offering their artifacts to the gallery to display and sell.

"Date: January 20, 1905

"Today was a very special day. I have renamed the gallery in honor of my father. From this day forward it will be known as 'The Jim Beaton Memorial Museum.'

"It wasn't to be a big event but a reporter from the Chicago Tribune showed up and took a picture of me holding an Indian Headdress. It was very embarrassing."

"That was her in the picture you found Lou," Virgil added.

"Date: October 24, 1929

"Today is a black day in Chicago. The Stock Market has crashed! People have been throwing themselves off the tops of buildings. Banks are closed and businesses are going under quickly. I only hope I can survive."

Lou had to explain what the Stock Market crash was and after he had finished all the Earps could do was shake their heads.

"Terrible times," Morgan added.

"Date: September 9, 1930

"My beautiful gallery will not survive. It has taken awhile but I must face the fact that I am soon to be penniless and the bank will close my doors in a matter of days."

"They're putting her out on the street?" Wyatt asked.

"Date: September 15, 1930

"This will be my last entry into these journals. My health is failing these days and I have been asked to leave my beloved gallery by day's end. I will be putting these ramblings of mine into the display case that contains Edwin's old western memorabilia and my father's keepsakes. They should be safe there. I believe that I now fall into that category and will soon become part of the history I tried so hard to preserve."

Lou noted that at the bottom of the last entry it was signed "Victoria Strong/Beaton of Chicago, Illinois; Deadwood, South Dakota and Tombstone Arizona."

Lou closed the journal and placed it on the table.

"That was one hell of a story Lou," Wyatt said.

"A sad one too," Lou added. "Victoria Beaton died a lonely, penniless woman and is buried in a pauper's grave on the north side of town. I'm going to visit that grave one of these days, to pay my respects and bury one of Bunny's and Millie's things next to her. I think she would like that."

Lou stood up to leave the Diner. "Well that's it Wyatt," Lou said. "That's how your gun got here after all this time and now I have it. You will have to come to terms with that. What do you say?"

Wyatt thought about it for a minute or so and finally said. "It's where it has to be, with an Earp."

With that Lou left the Diner and returned to the museum to replace Victoria's journals in the display case and look at the broken desk.

"I need a beer," he said to himself and left the museum.

Chapter 52

A few days had passed after the museum mystery had been solved and things were getting back to normal for Grimes. That is if you can call chasing bad guys normal.

He had taken a quick job from Abe and had just completed it with the help of his partners, the Earps and was settling down with his paper and a cold one when a small headline caught his eye, "POLICE ACTIVELY LOOKING FOR SIMMS MURDERER; REWARD OFFERED FOR ANY INFORMATION." Under the headline was a picture of Edith Simms.

Lou shook his head. "They just won't let it go," he thought. Lately he was beginning to wonder if Whitie's murder and the missing money would ever be put to rest but as luck would have it, people like money and it jogs their memories.

It didn't take long. A call came into Eddie's bar asking for Lou. He got off his stool and walked over to answer it, expecting it to be Abe offering him more work.

"Hello," he said.

The voice on the other end of the receiver spoke guardedly. "You Grimes?" he asked.

"Yeah I am," Lou replied.

"That reward still out there for the Simms thing?" he asked.

"Could be," Lou offered, "who's asking?"

"Edith Simms is alive and I can prove it," the voice said.

"I picked a lady up on Wallace and 5th two weeks ago she looked just like the picture in the newspaper. I took her to the airport."

Lou had heard all this before, just another asshole looking to score some quick dough with a bullshit story, then never to be seen again.

"How much is the reward?" the voice asked.

"$100 bucks for the right information," Lou offered "and a punch in the face for any lies you tell. Are you still interested Mac?"

"I'll be over in a half an hour," the voice said. "Have the hundred with you when I get there."

Lou hung up the phone and wasted no time in contacting Shamus at the Police Department.

"Do you think he's legit Lou?" Shamus asked.

"We will soon find out. Get your ass over here," he said.

Fifteen minutes later Shamus walked in the door and five minutes after that a heavy set man, about six foot tall walked into the bar and right up to Lou's stool.

Lou had never seen this man before but he knew what he was, a cabbie. You could tell right away by the cap he wore and the cabbie button that was attached to it.

"The name's Wally Burns," he said. "Are you Grimes?"

Lou nodded and pointed to his friend, "this here is Sergeant Shamus O'Hearn, one of Chicago's finest. He's here just in case you're trying to pull a fast one."

"No fast one," Burns said. "You got the money?"

Lou put the hundred on the bar, "your turn," he said.

Wally just shrugged his shoulders. "I knew who she was the first time I saw her picture in the paper but it was none of my business and I didn't want to get involved. I didn't put two and two together until after I read about the Simms guy and all that missing dough. She's gone Grimes," Wally said.

"I picked her up on the corner of Wallace and 5th and drove her around a bit, then she wanted me to take her to the Vanderbilt on Westmore Avenue, it's that high end ladies' store, and wait until she came out."

Shamus was taking notes all this time and listening intently.

"Go on Wally, what did she do next?" Lou asked.

"I waited like she wanted me to. Twenty minutes later she comes out of the store wearing the classiest pair of red shoes I've ever seen. Those babies were high class and big bucks. She noticed me looking at them and asked 'do you like em?' Oh, yes ma'am" I said. "They are top shelf all the way.

"'It's about me today,'" she said and then she asked me to drive her to the airport.

"I dropped her off and she gave me a big tip from the bag she was carrying. I told her to have a safe trip and she turned and walked into the airport.

"That was the last time I saw her until I saw her picture in the paper and the reward money. Here I am and here I go," said Wally as he reached for the hundred.

Lou put his hand on top of Burns' hand when he went for the money. "Don't forget to go down to the Police Station and write out a statement Wally. I've got your badge number if I have to come and find you."

Burns nodded his head and put the cash in his pocket. He turned to go then looked back at Lou and said "she's long gone guys, and so is all that cash."

Morgan and Wyatt were standing near, listening to everything. "Whitie's own mother stuck him and stole all that money," Morgan said. "These are really crazy times you live in cousin."

"We've got to check this out now Lou," Shamus said and was out the door without waiting.

"We're taking the squad car, it's easier to get to where we want to go, by using the siren," and they did.

They went first to the Vanderbilt boutique and confirmed that indeed a nice older lady had been in a couple of weeks ago and bought a very expensive pair of designer red high-heeled shoes.

Next they went to the airport and entered the main lobby. Shamus asked Lou how they were going to find out which airline Edith had taken.

"That's easy buddy," Lou said. "We start by asking the lady ticket sellers if they noticed a pair of high class red shoes go by them two or so weeks ago. Women notice stuff like that Shamus."

It took the guys maybe fifteen minutes to locate the ticket agent that sold a first class plane ticket to Edith for Florida, one-way.

"The shoes were stunning," she said.

Lou and Shamus looked at each other in disbelief. Edith got clean away and most likely would never be found.

"That's one for the books," Shamus said as they walked out of the terminal.

It was all that Lou could do to keep the Earps in check.

"You mean to say that people get into the belly of that steel monster? And it goes up in the air? Why?" Wyatt wanted to know. "Do they ever get out? Do they fall out of the sky? They actually pay money to walk into that monster's belly? No goddamn way, there's no goddamn way."

"For Christ's sake Shamus," Lou said, "Let's get out of here. I need a lot of beer."

Lou and Shamus arrived at Eddie's fifteen minutes later. They started talking about all that had transpired and determined the most logical sequence of events from everything they had found out from various places including Stella and the cabbie leading to and after Whitie's death.

Wally Burns was right when he said that Edith would never be found. There were enquiries, many enquiries, all of which led to dead end after dead end and in the end like any big city, life goes on.

The Simms' murder became another tragedy that sat at the bottom of a pending tray waiting to be filed if Edith was ever found.

Chapter 53

After Stella phoned Edith and told her that Whitie was at the track with a large amount of money she went immediately to her purse and found that her rent money was gone. Edith went cold. He was trying to put them both out on the street. This was the straw that broke the camel's back.

She went to a dark place in her mind. She was done with all of it. She put on her old grey coat with matching hat that had a small black feather off to the side. She put on red gloves, brown sensible shoes and a flowered scarf to block out the cold Chicago wind.

She left her toast and coffee where they were, on the kitchen table. She picked up her purse and left her apartment, locked the door behind her and never looked back.

She still had five cents in the bottom of her purse which she used to purchase a ticket on the trolley. In her purse, along with her pocketbook, a mirror to check herself in, an old brush to keep her hair in place from the blowing wind, a handkerchief, there was a nine inch razor sharp switchblade knife. Her father had carried it right up to the day he died and had shown Edith how to use it many times, and then he gave it to her and said "use it if you have to."

She got off the trolley a half block from the track and walked with the crowds up to the main doors and through the turnstiles. She blended right in and looked just like any other person going to the track that morning.

She entered the crowded main hall of the building and was quite surprised at how many people were there. She was just about to walk up to Stella's window when she saw Whitie stand up. "What was he doing on the floor?" she thought. "Who was that man on the floor next to him?" It didn't matter, nothing mattered right now.

She knew he didn't see her. This would have been the last place Whitie would have expected to see his mother and besides, he was too busy closing his bag. He had just finished closing it and appeared to be lost in thought. He looked up in Edith's direction and she could see the shock on his face, seeing her standing in front of him.

She could tell he was about to say something but never got the chance. Edith stepped in closer to administer the red hot searing blade into his upper right side that would stop him in his tracks. She could sense the numbness spreading over his body. She could see him fading away and then sensed a calmness that came over him. Her son was dead.

Edith knew exactly where to plunge the knife, the upper right side, just below the back's floating ribs. A full extension of the handle, then a twist and it was over.

As she watched the life leave his eyes, Edith had to act fast before they attracted attention. He was going down and she would not be able to hold him.

Just to her right was a bench that people used to read their racing forms before placing their bets. Her son began to crumble, she turned him quickly and his lifeless body landed in a sitting position on the end of the bench. To Edith's advantage, everyone around was too involved in placing bets and getting out to the track. She adjusted his body to look like he was resting, closed his trench coat and crossed his arms over his chest. The last thing she did was to adjust his hat so that he looked like he pulled it down to rest his eyes.

She sat for a few seconds making it look like she was talking to him then she picked up the bag and walked calmly out the door. She didn't look back, just blended into the crowds and walked down the street to wait for the next trolley.

She had been on the trolley for fifteen minutes before anybody even noticed that Whitie wasn't sleeping.

Edith was unaware of what happened next. A woman near him began to scream. A crowd gathered around the body before the police got there.

Whitie had slumped over on his side and a large amount of blood was seen from behind him. When the police arrived the crowd was pushed back so an investigation of the crime scene could be made.

There was nothing to see, only a dead man lying on a bench in the middle of a crowded building.

What the police didn't see in the crowd that formed was Donavon's four goons talking amongst themselves. They had gotten there too late and Ruby's thugs moving out the door in a rush to get to a phone.

Fifteen minutes had past and Edith had already left the trolley and was hailing a cab off the busy street after she noted the considerable amount of money that was in the bag she had taken from Whitie.

Chapter 54

Lou sat with the Earps at Eddies the following Saturday afternoon after the airport lead ended in defeat.

"That was one hell of a case cousin," Virgil said.

"I still can't believe it, Lou offered. "She just walked right out in front of us and we didn't see a thing.

"Abe phoned yesterday," Lou added. "He says he has a number of files that need our attention. Are you guys interested in sticking around? Or are you heading home now that the gun thing has been put to bed?"

The Earps looked at one another and Wyatt spoke first. "We're staying," he said. "The gun is here and so are you. Besides, you need us to keep you out of trouble and there is that Morgan question that needs to be answered. One more thing," he added, "when are you going to phone up that gal again? You know the one I'm talking about."

Lou was about to answer Wyatt by telling him it was none of his business when a man walked up behind him carrying a box.

"Are you Lou Grimes the Private Investigator?" he asked.

"Who's asking?" Lou wanted to know.

"Special delivery," the man answered.

Lou nodded, "I'm Grimes."

The delivery man put the box on the bar and walked away.

Lou sat for a minute looking at his special delivery.

"What do you think it is?" Virgil wanted to know.

"Well if it's a bomb, you won't have to worry about it," Lou joked and began opening the package.

When he finally got the box open and looked inside, he began to smile. "Well I'll be damned," he said, and lifted out a brand new hat!

Lou had to admit it was a beautiful hat and fit him to a T.

Wyatt looked at the box again and noticed it had a card inside. "Lou there's a card inside." He moved closer.

Grimes looked inside the box and picked up the card, read it, smiled and shook his head.

It simply said "I pay my debts, it's good for business."

Be sure to watch for the next book in the Lou Grimes Series "Tombstone Detective Agency – The Moors!"

Lou Grimes, ex-Chicago Police Detective has established himself as a new but credible gumshoe. His services are in demand and each case he takes on has an element of danger and challenge. Lou's alliance with his new found cousins, the Earps gives him a ghostly edge.

"'Kidnap my boys back for me from those evil bastards Mr. Grimes, by any means possible,' Diaz went on. 'I will make it worth your while. I can give you $1,000 now, $100 a day plus expenses and $10,000 when my boys are back home; that's $5,000 a piece. Then we part company and this matter goes away, never to be spoken of again.'

Silence filled the room and the Earps were watching the guards. Only the crackling of burning logs in the fireplace could be heard for some time.

'You know they're not going to come along quietly Constantine, don't you?' Lou finally opened up.

'Breathing Mr. Grimes; I want them both breathing, but I understand that sometimes unruly children need to have their asses slapped in order to get their attention. But breathing is the key word here.'"

Other books by Larry and Shirley Crandell:

The Tony Simons Series

- Branded
- Conquer the Hill
- Man of Honour

Non-fiction book by Shirley Crandell:

- Through the Fog

About the Authors!

Warrant Officer, Retired, Larry Edward Crandell, CD Medal; NATO Peacekeeping Medal; Gulf War Medal with Bar; Kuwait Liberation Medal; Order of St John's Medal.

Larry completed 25 years in the Canadian Military, working first on Radar Sites, then for NORAD as an Air Defence Technician. He then worked as a Nuclear Biological Chemical Defence Technician working for NATO in Germany. He is a Veteran of the Gulf War and was there when the night skies lit up as the missiles rained down on Bagdad. Larry spent many nights during the alerts alone in his shelter, out in the desert, writing journals about his experiences and wondering what he was doing there. He completed his military career as the Standards Warrant Officer at the Nuclear School in Borden Ontario.

Once retired from the military, he spent a few years working in the Alberta Tar Sands and teaching in Fort McMurray; he retired in Saskatoon, Saskatchewan and spends his time writing with his lovely wife of 38 years, Shirley.

Born on the prairies of Saskatchewan, Shirley's career of 35 years was in administration where she took to writing Newsletters and Standing Operating Procedures; and she has always enjoyed writing. She met Larry in 1980 and traveled the world with him and daughter Kathryn. Now retired, she has the time to spend on her personal passions, writing and jewelry making. She has previously published a non-fiction book called "Through the Fog."

Manufactured by Amazon.ca
Bolton, ON

27442057R00226